CU00869937

# GREAT ESCAPES

# VOLUME 1

# great escapes
## Volume 1

Edited by Chrissey Harrison

### Contributors
John H. Barnes, Andrew Campbell-Kearsey, Jim Cogan, Amy
Cummins, Troy Dennison, Damian Garside, Christopher M.
Geeson, Chrissey Harrison, Heidi Hovis, Sophie Jackson, T James,
Patti Ludwig, Drew Moffatt, Sabine Naus, Emma Scott, J. D. Waye,
Andy Whitson and Gareth Wilson.

### Illustrations
Kat Wilson

### Cover Photograph
Jeff Waye

great escape publishing

ISBN – 978-0-9575336-0-8

Printed and bound in the UK by
Imprint Digital

Also available in eBook format
ISBN – 978-0-9575336-1-5

**Great Escape Publishing**
thegreatesc.com/books
contact@thegreatesc.com

# CONTENTS

# ACKNOWLEDGEMENTS

The funds to print this book were raised through pre-orders placed through Kickstarter. We want to thank the following contributors who pledged £20 or more:

Matt Adams
Amy and Mark Adams
Daniel Cosser
Peter Drake
Jan Harrison
Heidi Hovis
Sophie Jackson
Rich
Steve McHugh
Terry of Wexford
Ben Staton
Andy Whitson
Matt Warner

And special thanks to
Simo Muinonen
For his generous contribution and for his creative input into the final story to be added to the anthology, *That Summer at the Lake.*

A full list if backers is available at
thegreatesc.com/hall-of-awesome

As Editor I would also like to thank Rich Jeffery for his support in all matters technical.

# ACKNOWLEDGEMENTS

The following works are reproduced in this anthology with the permission of the authors:

Poetry in my Pigeon Hole
© Copyright Andrew Campbell-Kearsey, 2012

Worst Valentines Night Ever © Copyright Jim Cogan, 2012

Broken Spirit, Reckless Love, Rise Above & Blood of the Moon
© Copyright Amy Cummins, 1997, 2011

Hunger Moon © Copyright Troy Dennison, 2011

One Corpse Too Merry © Copyright Christopher M. Geeson, 2011

Riverchild © Copyright Patti Ludwig, 2012

Paths © Copyright Drew Moffatt, 2012

Aftermath of a Stormy Night © Copyright T. James, 2011

Space: A Remorseless Calculated Inexactitude
© Copyright John H. Barnes, 2011

Starlight © Copyright Gareth Wilson, 2011

The Christmas Tights © Copyright Sabine Naus, 2011

Cat Nap © Copyright Damian Garside, 2011

The Cardinal Ruins © Copyright Heidi Hovis, 2011

Escape from the Night Terror © Copyright Emma Scott, 2012

Sagarmatha © Copyright J. D. Waye, 2011

Kiilling Time © Copyright Andy Whitson, 2012

Romance in White Gowns © Copyright Sophie Jackson, 2012

The cover image is used with the permission of the photographer:
Cover photograph © Copyright Jeff Waye 2011

# INTRODUCTION

The Editor

Great Escapes, Volume 1 is the first in a planned series of annual anthologies of short fiction and poetry. It features all the best fiction from the first year of The Great Escape, plus many new contributions. There are too many pieces in the book to mention each one individually here, but I'd like to share a little about how the book came together and a few highlights of its contents.

We start on the chilly slopes of Mount Everest with J. D. Waye's story *Sagarmatha*, inspired by the cover photograph which was taken by her brother, Jeff Waye, on the mountain itself. The photo was originally submitted simply to accompany the story, but as soon as I saw the amazing image I knew we had to have it for our cover.

The anthology includes our two contest winners from 2011/12, *One Corpse Too Merry* by Christopher M. Geeson and *Paths* by Drew Moffatt (originally published on the website under the pen name Matt Fewford). The runners up *The Christmas Tights* by Sabine Naus, *Poetry in my Pigeon Hole* by Andrew Campbell-Kearsey, *Romance in White Gowns* by Sophie Jackson and *Worst Valentine's Night Ever* by Jim Cogan also feature.

The competitions have been one of the most exciting parts of our journey into fiction publishing. For each great story we choose, we have to exclude two or three more, and that number grows with each new contest. Next year's anthology will feature the winners from our "Escape" micro fiction and poetry contest (two specially selected entries to which feature in this volume; *Killing Time* by Andy Whitson and *Escape from the Night Terror* by Emma Scott), and the winners of our "(Un)Conventional" short story contest, held in March 2013 to celebrate the launch of Volume 1.

Some of our favourite contributions have come from direct submissions or chance offers, including Troy Dennison's *Hunger Moon*, Patti Ludwig's *Riverchild* and Heidi Hovis' *The Cardinal*

*Ruins.* Next year we plan to include many more pieces of this type by opening up our call for submissions more publicly.

The book concludes with a brand new short story written specifically for this anthology; *That Summer at the Lake.* Print publication of this book was made possible by our Kickstarter backers who pre-ordered their copies. As part of the campaign, we offered up the chance to choose the theme and plot of the final story. Simo Muinonen snapped up the reward and then came up with a great original idea for me to write. Hopefully I did it justice; you'll have to read to find out.

At the back of the book you'll find biographies for our contributors. Many include titles of their other published works and web links so you can find out more.

I hope you enjoy reading this book as much as I enjoyed putting it together. See you next year for Volume 2!

# GREAT ESCAPES
# VOLUME 1

# SAGARMATHA

J. D. Waye

Stone monuments to the dead line the path to Everest. There's no way past them, no moving beyond the reminder that one in four people will die in the attempt to summit and return. I remember resting a hand on those rough stones, breathing a muted prayer to the souls that walked this route before me. The little colourful flags danced in the breeze. Fog hung heavy, obscuring and softening the verdant valley.

That was the last time I saw colour. It seems fitting that in my final moment, those prayer flags would be the image lingering in my mind.

Whiteness. Nothing but shades of white – swirling, dancing, colliding and hammering against my face. I reached into my pocket for a cigarette. I'd promised to give them up, but it didn't really matter anymore. Pungent tobacco bit through air so thin and sterile, it wouldn't carry any scent I didn't bring along with me: fear, sweat, laundry soap, wet wool.

Fingers stiff and white, the blackening notes of frostbite forming on the tips, I fumbled with the lighter. It snapped and sparked, finally bearing a pathetic flame. I sucked at my smoke, gave my butt to the wind, and tucked my stubby digits into my mitts. I cursed my bad luck, my stupidity, my physical inadequacies; the guide who abandoned me.

There was no point to going on. I was lost, and left behind. So much for Joe's promise to get me home. My fault, for choosing to climb without canned air. The guide made the right decision: sacrifice the idiot, spare the team. A quiet comfortable sleepiness stole over me. No pain, no drama. A gentle surrender.

"Mister Alex. Wake up. Come now."

I raised my head and rubbed my eyes. "Sherpa Joe. You came back for me."

"Yes."

"Where's everybody else?"

"Down below," he said. I shuffled along in his wake, the hunched form of his backpack making him look misshapen. He paused whenever I lagged behind, and waved a hand. "Not far now."

The black-white sky flashed. Thunder rumbled, echoing into the longer chaos of another avalanche. Fear paralysed my limbs, shutting me down, until Joe's words broke the spell.

"Hurry. Not far now."

I clung to his voice, the only shred of sanity in the swirling blizzard.

The air thickened as we descended. My lungs gratefully sucked in the extra oxygen. Muscles burned in fatigue; I wanted to lie down and quit. But hope won when the humped forms of tents rose from windswept rock. We'd made it all the way past Camp Four, down to Camp Three. I'd been too tired to notice the passing of the time. It could have been an hour, or the whole night. My headlamp winked out, battery dead.

"Now you can sleep," Sherpa Joe said, as he unzipped my tent.

I gripped his hand. Tears stung my eyes, wasted moisture in my dehydrated, delirious state. "Thank you for coming back for me."

"I promised you, Mister Alex. I swore on Sagarmatha. Now put your hands like this." He stuffed his fingers into his armpits.

I wondered where everyone else was, why it was so quiet. No sounds of snoring, talking, swearing; no drone of radio cutting the silence. They must all be exhausted beyond belief. I crawled into the warm cocoon of my sleeping bag, and let go of the world.

The moisture in my breath clung to the insides of the tent, snowing down when I bumped my head against the canvas. My fingers hurt. I tugged at the mitts, afraid to look, but they weren't any worse than yesterday. Maybe I'd get to keep them.

Pristine white greeted me everywhere I looked; barely a sign of our tents popped up sun-bleached red and khaki between drifts. The campsite was deserted – not even marred by track marks of the quiet, competent Sherpa Joe.

I couldn't find my lighter, but there was a spare in somebody else's pack. I lit a fire on the campstove, melted some water, and shovelled a can of cold beans down my throat. Bland and tasteless, like the water.

I waited the whole day, alone, while the mountain hung silent and brooding. The weather was perfect for climbing, inviting, like a Venus fly trap, alluring, beautiful, welcoming – until it snaps down its jaws.

The last rays of sunlight bathed the peaks in glowing orange and pink. I slept fitfully, the wind howling spirit sounds, tangling and invading my dreams. Agony, pain, all mixed up in a haunting melody.

The loneliness was oppressive; I could not endure another day in this stark solitude. I packed up my few things, rolled up my sleeping bag, and headed down for Base Camp. It was frightening being alone again, lost like before Joe found me, my mortality dangling with each tentative footstep and handgrip. The mountain reigned like a living menace, eyes boring into my back, sending rocks and boulders tumbling as if to hurry me off the barren slopes.

Shattered nerves, shaking hands, eyes burning from the glare, but I made it. The tang of unwashed bodies rose on the breeze. Pots clattered, voices rose and fell; music buzzed on a radio.

Silence descended as all eyes fell on me. I could understand the shocked expressions – I'd been written off as another casualty of arrogance. But where were my friends, my team mates? The guide who left me behind? Where was Sherpa Joe?

They'd all perished in the avalanche that took out Camp Four. While I was having my pity party on the ridge, they were gasping their last breaths under a crushing blanket of snow. The bodies were retrieved, one by one, lined up for identification. Arms cradling skulls, legs curled; fear, horror, resignation etched on frozen faces. And there was Sherpa Joe, my cigarette lighter in his pocket, the only one peaceful like a sleeping child.

There are plenty of ways to explain what happened, and they all involve human error. Maybe I was wrong about seeing Sherpa Joe. He couldn't have come back for me – he was already dead. Maybe it was my imagination, bizarre hallucinations from the dehydration and fatigue, the lack of oxygen messing with my brain. Maybe the radio dispatcher got the times wrong, or the translator got some of the words mixed up.

But I saw Joe standing next to the stone monuments, a smile lighting up his earnest, serious face. He faded away as I drew near. He'd made a promise to me – an oath on his sacred Sagarmatha – and he hadn't failed to get me home.

I grabbed a rock, the biggest one I could lift, and started building Joe his own monument. Rest in peace, my friend.

# RISE ABOVE

Amy Cummins


My openness was my downfall.
His arrogance was his.
My honesty
And devotion
Were made into unworthy traits,
Were used as weapons to attack me.
His vanity
And conceitedness
Were made into admirable qualities,
Were used to humiliate me.
But I shall rise above it,
For he is beneath my contempt.

# NO WAY HOME

Chrissey Harrison


One day, Sophie stepped through a door into a green meadow beside a village. The door vanished behind her.

"What do I do now?" she asked the sky.

"Find another door," a voice on the wind replied.

Well, the door to the local pub seemed a good place to start.

# POETRY IN MY PIGEON HOLE

Andrew Campbell-Kearsey

"Well, something's put a spring in your step."

Roger chose to ignore his secretary's comment and closed the door to his office behind him. He sat at his desk and took out a folded piece of blue writing paper from his left jacket pocket.

He straightened the paper out on his desk and reread the four lines. He was ashamed to admit that he was no poetry expert. As a headmaster, some people would perhaps have expected him to have strong opinions on the matter. Roger couldn't tell his Keats from his Shelley. He found any modern stuff to be pointless.

But this was different. In four bare lines, the writer simply informed him that he was the reason she came to work. It was the essence of him that enabled her to get through the day. He gave meaning to her humdrum existence. It was all terribly flattering, but who was his admirer?

He was accustomed to badly punctuated written requests by staff, with pathetic pleas for time off. He had never received anything like this before. He speculated about the writer of this poem. The purple inked italic script did not betray the writer's identity. There were several members of staff that he would like it to be, yet many more he would not want cast in the role of head teacher's admirer.

For one awful moment he worried that Phil in the science department had chosen this particular time to come out, and that he had chosen his line manager as the misplaced object of his affection. Looking at the poem again, the writer clearly referred to '*her* beating heart.' So, unless Phil was also considering gender reassignment, Roger's admirer was female.

His phone rang and he answered. It was his secretary informing him that his deputy wanted to see him. Brenda could wait, he thought. He knew what she would say anyway. She would go on about how she'd reorganised the staffroom and tidied some shelves. It was all too boring for words.

As a new head teacher, he had inherited Brenda from his predecessor. Roger had quickly assessed that the best thing for him to do was to shield parents and children from her incompetence. Unfortunately she wasn't guilty of sackable offences. So he gave her little projects.

Her recent challenge had been to spruce up the staffroom and communal areas. He had given her a shoestring budget and she had taken up the gauntlet with considerable, yet irritating enthusiasm.

Unfortunately for Roger, she was keen to share all developments with her boss. Her most recent dilemma was whether she should group the teaching magazines in the staffroom by theme or title. Roger had heard last week about her constant fight to maintain a whole set of working white board marker pens. He couldn't face it this morning.

"Tell her I'm busy."

He reread his love poem a few more times. For the first time in weeks he was smiling.

After lunchtime, he went through to the empty staffroom to make himself a coffee. At the sink, he glanced over at the staff pigeonholes at the other side of the room. Roger glimpsed another folded piece of blue writing paper that matched the previous missive.

He rushed over to retrieve it. In his haste he forgot he was carrying his hot drink. He tripped on the leg a low table in the middle of the room and the contents of his mug was spilt over the magazines. He was dabbing at them with some paper towels when Brenda entered.

"Oh dear, what a mess and I've only just tidied them."

She walked over to Roger and took the soggy coffee-stained paper towels out of his hands and got down on her hands and knees, saying, "Don't worry headmaster, I'll clear this up."

Roger took Brenda at her word and exited swiftly, taking the now familiar blue paper from his pigeonhole.

Back in his office, he read the latest instalment. It didn't disappoint. The writer extolled his many manly attributes and longed for the time that they could be together as one. Roger was concerned that she was coming on a little too strong, however welcome the attention was.

Roger had a meeting of the governing body that evening and he was attempting to put the finishing touches to his head teacher's report. Usually this activity was simple for him; he just listed the school's achievements, staff appointments and attached the latest budget statement. But he was unable to concentrate on the task.

He phoned his secretary to come through so that he could dictate some letters.

She sat poised with her pad and pen but the normally loquacious man was short on words today. After he struggled to compose a simple letter to the parents of a persistent truant, she leaned forward in her chair and asked, "whatever's the matter Roger?"

He was normally a very private man. However he needed a second opinion about the letters and a course of action. He reached into his drawer, retrieved the two pieces of blue paper and handed them to her.

She put down her pad and read the letters. She obviously knew this was no laughing matter from the way he was taking it all very seriously.

"Who do you think it could be?"

"Well, I have my suspicions but I'm reluctant to say at the moment as I may be proved wrong."

"Perhaps you should encourage this mystery woman to show her hand?"

"How can I do that?"

"Well there is the end of term staff meal approaching and perhaps this time you shouldn't leave early like you always do."

"I like to let the staff let their hair down and relax which must be difficult with me around."

"I don't think you should flatter yourself into thinking that the staff see you as a Ghengis Khan figure."

"I don't know whether to take that as an insult or a compliment."

They agreed that it would be too obvious if Roger kept popping into the staffroom to check the contents of his pigeonhole. His secretary agreed to collect his notes and mail.

The very next morning, before the school day had begun, she rushed into his office without knocking. She knew that Roger was alone.

"There's another note on the same blue paper, but this time it's not in your pigeonhole but Philip's. It looks like your admirer is either two-timing you or keeping her options open."

Roger got up out of his chair and walked into the staffroom. His secretary followed closely behind. He stood in front of the pigeonholes, pointing at the new letter on blue paper and turned to her.

"Don't be so daft. There it is, in *my* pigeonhole."

She tapped at the name on the label beneath his pigeonhole. "I do wish you'd wear your glasses. That used to be your pigeonhole until Brenda rearranged them last week and put them into alphabetical order by first name. She seemed to think it would foster a more informal atmosphere in the workplace.

"As you can see it is now Philip's. So I am sorry to disappoint you Roger but it seems as if he is the one with a mystery admirer. Something tells me that whoever she is, she is going to be heartbroken when he finally decides to come out. I saw him a few weekends ago out shopping with his partner. He didn't see me, but they looked ever so happy together. Hope it lasts."

Brenda chose that moment to come into the staffroom and saw Roger and his secretary in front of the pigeonholes.

"Just admiring your handiwork, Brenda. You're making a lovely job of the staffroom."

His deputy blushed.

"Sorry I can't stop to chat, Brenda, but I have some letters to dictate."

Back in his office, he handed the two love poems to his secretary.

"Please can you do me a huge favour and place these in Philip's pigeonhole."

"Of course. One more thing Roger. May I book you an optician's appointment?"

# BROKEN SPIRIT

Amy Cummins

Bound eternally,
To a man I now distrust.
Forever tied,
To a man who broke my spirit.
This man,
Once the most important
Person in my life,
Has conspired to destroy
What remained of my soul.

# THE CHRISTMAS TIGHTS

Sabine Naus

"I'm going to get more stocking stuffers than you," boasted seven-year-old Daphne to her friend, as they played in the backyard.

They had just finished making a snowman and were surveying their handiwork. The snowman's eyes were two crusty old chestnuts left behind by a squirrel. Thin twigs created eyebrows. An icicle served as the nose and the mouth was simply an upward arch made by Daphne's index finger.

"How do you know? Santa has to give everyone the same." Shanna frowned as she lay down to make a snow angel.

"Na, uh. I know how to get more stuff because I've got a plan." Daphne lay down beside her and began to wave her arms.

The two little girls laughed when their mittened hands touched. The sky above them was a crisp blue and they had to squint against the brightness of the sun.

"I still don't believe you," said Shanna, getting up and banging her snow crusted mittens together.

"I'll tell you my secret." Daphne's eyes danced. "But you have to promise not to tell anyone else."

Shanna was immediately interested and bobbed her head up and down as they headed towards Daphne's house for some hot chocolate and biscuits.

"Tonight, after mom and dad go to bed, I'm taking my stocking down and hanging up my tights because they can hold much more stuff. They're stretchy and long."

Shanna looked impressed. "Wow, that's a great idea."

"But you can't steal my idea." Daphne was serious. "And you can't tell anyone either."

"My tights have a hole in them," stated Shanna, quite matter-of-factly. "And I'm your bestest friend so I won't tell a soul." For emphasis, she placed a finger over her mouth.

"Good plan, eh?" Daphne felt excited. She was going to get more stuff than her brother and sister and all of her friends because she'd come up with a great plan.

"If I get a new pair of tights next year, can I do it too?" asked Shanna, suddenly wishing she'd had such a great idea first.

"Of course! Santa will be used to it by then." The two girls took off their coats and boots, letting their damp mittens dangle on the strings wound through each of their parkas, and hurried to the kitchen where a treat awaited them.

Daphne heard her parents go into their bedroom and quickly tiptoed out into the hallway. It was dark but there was a full moon shining through the landing window so she had some light as she carefully made her way down the carpeted stairs to the living room.

She knew Santa never came before midnight and since she could tell the time, she knew her plan was going to work. The houses outside were still lit up and the colourful lights could be seen blinking through the sheer curtains.

Daphne's stocking was the one next to her mother's. Her father's was first and after hers came the last two stockings; one for her brother, Toby and the other for her sister, Dixie. Quietly, she removed her red felt stocking from its peg and replaced it with her pair of white tights. She stood back and smiled. Already she could imagine the wonderful amount of surprises she would get from Santa.

With the red Christmas stocking tucked in one hand, she hurried back to her bedroom hoping morning would come soon.

"What's this?" Tristan had just turned on the living room lights and spotted the pair of tights.

His wife, Delia, chuckled. "What on earth is Daphne thinking?" She picked up the tights and shook her head.

The husband and wife were about to play Santa and arrange the Christmas gifts under the tree as well as fill up the stockings.

"She's being greedy." A sly smile appeared on his face. He took the tights, stretched them out and laughed. "You know she's expecting these to be filled up."

They looked at each other and both stifled a bout of laughter for fear of waking their children.

"I have an idea." Tristan winked at Delia and, as they began to set up the gifts, he whispered his idea to her.

When Daphne opened her eyes Christmas morning, she gleefully bounded out of bed.

"Merry Christmas!" she sang out as she rushed into Toby's room first and then into Dixie's. Toby was already awake and sitting up in bed. Dixie was still curled up under her blanket.

"Merry Christmas!" shouted Toby and he and Daphne shook Dixie's bed. Startled, the little girl raised her head and gaped at them through sleep hazed eyes.

"Get up! It's Christmas!" Toby was hopping from one foot to another. "I'm going to get Mom and Dad."

Daphne threw back Dixie's covers and took the three-year-old by the hand.

"Let's go see what Santa brought."

"Santa, Santa, Santa," repeated Dixie, eyes widening in anticipation.

Toby was singing *We Wish You a Merry Christmas* at the top of his lungs and she could hear her parents groaning. Dad moaned that it was only the crack of dawn and Mom was begging for ten more minutes of sleep.

But, Toby was relentless, and finally the family was gathered together in the living room.

While Tristan plugged in the lights for the tree, Delia prepared coffee in the kitchen. She knew the kids were too excited to eat but she and her husband needed the coffee.

Once they had their mugs in hand, they sat down to watch their children who were all lined up on their knees in front of the twinkling tree.

"Stockings first," announced Delia, sharing a secretive look with Tristan. "Daphne, you hand out the stockings please."

Daphne's eyes were huge when she spotted her bulging tights. There was even a big red bow on one foot! After giving each their stocking, she sat down on the floor, eager to open hers.

"Hey, there's nothing in mine." Toby turned his stocking upside down. "It's empty."

"Me too," added Dixie, shaking hers several times.

Daphne watched as her parents opened their stockings and also found nothing. Suddenly she didn't feel so good.

"What's in your stocking?" asked her father.

A lump prevented her from speaking, so silently she opened the top of the tights.

"Wow, look at all the stuff Santa got her!" The corners of Toby's mouth dipped down and for an instant, she thought her five-year-old brother was going to cry. Tears already glistened in Dixie's eyes as she grappled to get into her mother's lap.

"Show us, Daphne," urged Tristan, gathering his son into his arms.

Face flaming, she reached in and first pulled out five gingerbread men. They were followed by five oranges, five candy canes, five small bags of gumdrops, five identical knit hats and five balls. That was a lot of stuff.

Ashamed, she looked up at her family and then back down at the array of treasures. Suddenly she brightened.

"There's one for each of us!" She cried out in delight and began to hand one of everything to each member of the family.

"That's right." Tristan's eyes met Delia's.

"I guess Santa was in a hurry and stuffed them all into yours," explained Toby thoughtfully, before biting the head off his gingerbread man.

Daphne could only nod. She was feeling very humble and very embarrassed. How could she have been so greedy? Her plan hadn't been a good one.

Sensing her unease, Delia slipped onto the floor and pulled her into a hug. "Merry Christmas, Sweetie Pie!"

"Ho, ho, ho!" chortled Dixie. Toby and Tristan joined in as the family opened the remaining gifts together.

## UMBRELLA

Chrissey Harrison

The clear plastic umbrella lay broken on the side of the road. Twisted and forlorn. It looked so sad. Unloved.

And, it wasn't exactly keeping the rain off any more; cold rain that drove in at an angle.

Never mind, it's not mine, I thought, as the bus pulled away.

# THE DIARY OF JOSEPH MORTIMER

Chrissey Harrison

*In June 2010 a freak fire gutted a 16<sup>th</sup> Century farmhouse in Hampshire. During the renovation following the disaster the owners found, concealed beneath the floorboards, the diary of one Joseph Mortimer; a thirty-seven year old land owner of modest holdings, who died in 1583. The details of his fate are vague and his body was never found.*

*Below is presented the final entry. The language has been updated somewhat, but an effort has been made to preserve the flavour of the piece.*

1st November 1583
At the home of Mr John Milner
Breamore, Hampshire, ENGLAND

The events of this night have been disturbing and traumatic. Were it not for the blood still staining my hands I would think it all a nightmare. But I am getting ahead of myself, I should tell the whole story. I will try to record exactly what happened.

The night started out with a strange visit. While my dear wife Catherine laid the children in their beds, there was a knock at the door. Perhaps not cause for alarm on any other night, but on the night of Samhain things are not always as they seem. I was not about to invite a stranger into my home. Cautiously, I opened the door.

"Good sir, might I be so bold as to beg a crust of bread, and the warmth of your fire for a time?"

On my doorstep stood a woman, or at least that is what she appeared. Her filthy grey hair hung lank in her face and she was dressed in layers of rags. The yellow stumps of her few remaining teeth flashed at me as she attempted to smile. I recoiled, covering my nose against her stench.

"Be gone woman, I have not the space or the food to spare. There is an inn at Fordingbridge."

"Good sir, I have come from Fordingbridge, on the road to Salisbury. Please, I ask only scraps and perhaps an hour to rest my tired old legs. Perhaps you have a barn?"

"And have your stench spook my horses, I think not."

"Those with no generosity in their hearts eventually realise that a little charity is a small price to pay to guard against losing more than they can afford."

I blinked, baffled by her riddle and then shook my head. "I'm sorry, but you will have to continue on your way and try your luck elsewhere."

I closed the door and thought no more about it. Catherine and I retired to our beds not long after.

A second knock at my door, a frantic pounding, woke me from my slumber scarcely two hours later. My eyes bleary with sleep, I lit a candle and went to investigate the commotion.

Standing in the crisp cold night, a single lantern between them, stood my two farm hands. Young Henry looked white as a sheet. His shock of bright ginger hair looked almost red in the candle light. Beside him Christopher, a little older and wiser, worried at a hangnail with his teeth. Something had frightened them.

"There is something in the stable, sir," Christopher said. "The horses are fretting."

"What kind of thing?" I asked, reluctant to leave the warmth of the house.

"I don't know sir, but they are stamping and pulling at their tethers."

They would not be satisfied until I looked with them. I pulled on my britches, boots and coat, lit another lantern from my candle, and followed them into the darkness.

In the stables the horses snorted and stamped, their hides glossy with a sheen of sweat. Sweat from fear. As I approached my mare, Jubilee, she reared, her eyes rolling. The only time I had ever seen the horses like this was when a rabid dog had been loose on the farm.

A faint scratching reached my ears. I bade the lads hold the horses steady, so I could listen, and traced the sound to a mound of hay in one corner. As I approached, the mound rustled. I took a pitchfork from the rack on the wall and stepped slowly closer. With the tines of the fork I gently moved the top layer of hay.

An enormous rat leapt from the mound and darted for the door. My heart raced from the shock but I quickly recovered myself. Just a rat. Although, it was strange for the horses to fret so over a mere rat.

"I see it," Henry said. "It made for the grain store."

He hurried towards the door and Christopher followed him. I grumbled to myself that the problem could be investigated in the morning - rts were always a problem around harvest time - but they were already half way across the yard.

The rat from the stable stood boldly by the door to the grain store. It was almost as if it wanted to be followed and was waiting for us to catch up. I pushed past the lads and opened the door. As our light flooded into the pitch black space a number of small furry bodies scattered to the sides and disappeared.

Scratching and chittering sounds came from every side but I could see no rats. Sacks of grain were piled high. It had been a good harvest this year and the mill was struggling to cope. My grain would not go to the mill for another week. If there was a problem with rats it could all be ruined by then.

I hung my lantern on a hook by the door and set about searching the edges. Henry and Christopher followed my lead, searching the opposite side of the room. The sound of rats seemed to be everywhere.

"Here," Henry said, suddenly. "Behind this sack!"

Before I could stop him he reached for the corner of a sack near the bottom of the pile and wrenched it. The bag split and the grain spilled onto the floor. I held my breath for a moment as the sacks above settled into the gap that was forming. Another sack started to slip sideways, a third ripped open, and then the whole stack started to move, toppling forwards.

Rats appeared from everywhere, springing from the stack of grain from the top to the bottom, some flying through the air as they leapt. There must have been hundreds. Their warm little bodies brushed past my legs, claws scrabbling on the smooth stone floor.

Henry, standing closest to the stack, cried out as sack dislodged from the top and struck him on the shoulder. Before Christopher or I could react the slide engulfed him.

I felt a tug on my britches and a sharp pain. I looked down to see one of the creatures climbing up me, its sharp claws piercing my skin. I shuddered and struck it away. Another leapt at me from the stack and clamped its teeth into the flesh of my hand. I backed towards the door as more rats swarmed towards me. Across the room Christopher tried to fend off rats with a broom.

The dust from the fall settled and I could finally make out the prone form of Henry, pinned beneath the grain. The fingers of his one free arm dripped with blood as he frantically beat away the attacking rats. As I watched, one darted in and took a bite from his cheek. Christopher tried to make his way to Henry but the rats swarmed and forced him back towards the door. I am ashamed to admit I stood frozen with fear.

Henry's screams became more frantic and I watched in horror as two rats clamped onto his hand, only falling back to the floor when his fingers detached. One eye was already a bloody pit, but the other found mine, pleading and terrified. Then he disappeared under a writhing mass of fur and needle teeth, and screamed no more.

Bile rose in my throat as Christopher dragged me through the door into the biting cold of the night. When I recovered my senses, I realised they were no longer attacking us. They were streaming across the yard, moving all as one, towards the house. Towards Catherine and the Children.

"Get Jubilee into the trap," I instructed Christopher. He nodded and hurried back towards the stable to harness the horse.

I ran to the house. There were rats everywhere and I struggled to keep my balance when my foot came down on a small furry back instead of hard ground.

I managed to overtake the flood so that when I reached the door I had time to get through and close it before the tide struck. I backed away slowly. From outside the sounds of scrabbling claws and gnawing teeth was punctuated with soft thuds as the rats hurled their small bodies against the door. This was unnatural. But then, this was a night for unnatural things.

"Joseph?" Catherine's voice from behind.

I fought down the rising panic and turned to her. "Get the children, we have to go."

"Go where? Why?"

"Please Catherine, there's no time."

Her eyes widened and her face paled but she nodded and turned towards the children's room.

The scratching and scraping came from all sides now. The windows, the eves... under the floorboards. We had only minutes until they found a way in. I picked up the fire iron and held it ready.

Catherine returned holding little Sarah by the hand. My daughter held her rag doll in her other hand. Edward followed behind, too old now for holding his mother's hand. He rubbed his eyes and stifled a yawn.

"What is that noise?" Catherine asked, her voice trembling, her gaze darting around.

"Rats."

Sarah's eyes widened and her face paled. At that moment a faint tinkling from the kitchen signalled a window pane had succumbed to the onslaught. Within seconds the first whiskered nose appeared around the door. Sarah screamed, dropped her mother's hand and bolted for her bedroom. Catherine went after her.

Outside I heard the welcome sound of hooves on the courtyard stone. Moments later Christopher pounded on the door. I opened it and found him fending rats off the path with a broom. A couple slipped past into the house. It was incidental, we weren't staying. I handed Edward the fire iron and told Christopher to get him to the trap while I went back.

In the children's bedroom Sarah had crawled into a wall cupboard and would not come out. I crouched next to Catherine

"She's frightened. She has nightmares about rats," she said.

I knew why, although I did not think she remembered. She was barely two years old at the time. I had come home early one afternoon when the rain had halted work in the fields and found a huge rat in her basket, perched on her infant chest.

A small weight landed on my shoulder and hissed in my ear. I threw it off and turned to see half a dozen rats creeping closer, their backs bristling, teeth bared.

"Pull her out, I'll keep them away," I said to Catherine and aimed a swift kick at the leading rat.

Catherine pulled Sarah from the cupboard, with much difficulty as our daughter did not want to be moved. I lead the way back to the door, trying to clear a path. Catherine came last, forcing Sarah to keep moving.

The scene that greeted us at the door seemed like something from the ten plagues of Egypt. Jubilee, tethered to the gate, was a hair's breadth from breaking her rope and bolting. Her legs were bloody from rat bites. In the trap behind her Edward darted about clearing rats from the wheels as they tried to climb up. Christopher, his shirt soaked in blood from a hundred tiny wounds valiantly kept the way clear.

I paused and swept Sarah up into my arms to carry her to the trap. I crossed the threshold with Catherine on my heels.

I had barely gone two steps when my wife screamed. Rats dropped from the eves, so many they weighed her down. I could not stop; I had to get Sarah to the trap. My heart broke as I turned my back and continued forward.

Christopher fought his way to Catherine and tried to free her but his strength was failing. A rat dropped onto his back and sank its teeth into his ear. He dropped the broom which was immediately swallowed up by the writhing mass. By the time I reached the trap and passed Sarah to Edward he was on his knees.

Catherine curled up in a ball, trying to protect her face and stomach. I didn't know what to do. Jubilee danced in her tracers, foaming at the mouth. If the rope broke, Edward would not have the strength to hold her.

As I glanced back one last time Christopher cried out and threw his head back. I stared, unable to tear my gaze away as sharp rodent teeth dug into the flesh of his neck and ripped it open. Blood sprayed and he slumped forward with a stomach churning sound that was part way between a gurgle and a hiss.

THE DIARY OF JOSEPH MORTIMER

As the drops of his warm blood fell on the writhing hoard they seemed to go into a frenzy. Catherine screamed and jerked as the mass descended. For a moment I could not see her and then a gap opened. What I saw then caused my stomach to heave and I vomited acid bile into the bushes. Her white linen night dress was shredded and red with blood, the flesh below a morbid pulp exposing white bone. She was still moving, but it would not be for long.

At that moment Jubilee reared and the trap jumped forward a pace. Hot tears coursed down my cheeks as I climbed into the trap and urged the horse forwards. Behind me Sarah screamed for her mother. Edward openly wept, although he sat stoically upright, holding his sister.

I did not push Jubilee too hard; she was already weak from fear and loss of blood. The children's cries died down to a quiet plaintive murmur, and then silence as they fell asleep in each other's arms.

Some two miles down the road I passed a figure huddled at the side of the road in tattered rags.

"Had some trouble, good sir?" she cackled as we passed. Her laughter continued to ring in my ears for some time. Witch! She had brought this curse down on me and mine.

And so I find myself here, in the home of my good friend John Milner. They kindly took us in and tended our wounds. John's wife took Sarah and Edward and settled them in to sleep with their children some half an hour ago.

As luck would have it my diary was in the pocket of my coat and so I resolved to record the events as best I could, lest no one believe me when the dawn comes. I can scarcely believe it myself but the memory is so clear. It is almost as if I can hear the scratching of the rats at my door right now...

# AFTERMATH OF A STORMY NIGHT

T. James

Roiling inside, she boils like pitch.

Once sensuous, caressing; now seething, enveloping;

White silks' soft seductions torn and re-sewn into her black
gravid cloak folds;

Wreathed around her in the vain pursuit of solace, they just seal
in the cold.

The slighted mistress' vindictive rage is unleashed in an envious
ejaculation of impotent hate,

A transient sonic satiation, its hollow echoes reverberating to
nothing.

Time after time, the very earth trembles,

But her vainglorious heart remains unappeased.

Where once lovers' soft whispers caressed,

The gentlest of stolen touches hardened to unseen ebon-painted
talons,

That picked, plucked, ensnared.

Now venting her unrequited fury, howling, she rends any and all
she touches –

Heedless of the broken lives she leaves behind.

# AFTERMATH OF A STORMY NIGHT

Silvered electric arc-lights play in her indigo hair,
Callous barbed pins hypnotizing entranced watchers,
Fixating them like moths to her collector's board.
After-images play across the velvet undulating contours of her
    cloaked breast,
Each an incandescent reflection of her caprice.


Yet Time permeates all,
And pours forth an unrelenting deluge of Justice from which there
    is no sanctuary.
It gathers, into a swollen torrent, seeking to bear her away,
As alone, reviled, she shelters foetally in the bed she failed to
    make,
Her cloak sodden with love's lost cold, bitter tears.

# PATHS

Drew Moffatt

The bar is actually *called* Arrows. Big, neon-lit white letters, cursive and flowing to the point of near-illegibility, on a sickening deep pink background dotted with squint-to-see-em red hearts. On each window, they've etched an ornate, fragile-looking bow nocked with an arrow that has a heart-shaped head. It's embarrassing.

As I stand in line, I wonder if the bar's "romantic" theme was designed in earnest. If it was, the owners must have been disappointed to find out that if you invite people to come looking for love at your establishment, what they actually come looking for is sex. There *is* a difference. I'd be out of a job if there wasn't.

More likely, the proprietors knew exactly what they were doing. Sex is what sells, after all. Maybe the lightless alley that runs up the side of the place is supposed to be a feature, not a shady inconvenience.

I get to the door and pay the cover charge. The bouncer barely notices me, which is the intended effect. The unremarkable brunette he sees on my arm may or may not be real; she will dissolve into the crowd once we're inside, and continue to make no impression on anyone.

There *is* love to be found here, believe it or not, and good love. The forever kind. You just have to be good at spotting it. And that's what I do; that's what I've done all my life. I've become an expert at it. I spotted it here.

The two I've spotted don't know each other yet. He's over at the bar waiting for his change, and she's sitting at a table alone, pretending to do something with her phone.

She's here with her friends. Rachel phoned her at four this afternoon, and said *of course* she had to come out this evening, because Sarah's in town for the weekend and Sarah just broke up with Simon, so *of course* they're all going out to Arrows to help her get over it. She thinks it's a stupid idea, really. She doesn't really know what Sarah needs to help her deal with her breakup, but she's pretty sure it's not a one-night-stand with a stranger at a singles bar. (She's right.)

Now Rachel and Sarah have gone off to find the toilets, and she's been left to guard their table, and their coats. Alone and self-conscious, she pretends to be texting so that she doesn't look quite so... pathetic.

He's here on his own because he's lonely and desperate and a little naïve. He works in an office, lives in a one-bedroom flat and spends his life moving back and forth from one to the other every few hours. He owns one ill-fitting second-hand suit, and one battered second-hand briefcase, because he's not an important person at the company.

And it doesn't matter what *he* looks like, and it doesn't matter what *she* looks like. I spotted it here.

Well, to be technical, I spotted it somewhere else, some *when* else. They'll never know it, but they'd met before tonight. Three days ago he was at work, sitting in his little blue cubicle, and she'd walked past his door. They hadn't seen each other's faces. She'd seen his ratty, scuffed briefcase for a moment as she'd passed. In it, she'd seen the corner of the cover of some dopey thriller that he was reading and she'd read before and liked. He'd looked up as she walked on, and all he'd seen was the shoe on her trailing foot before it vanished behind carpeted blue wall, and he'd thought it was a pretty shoe.

They'll meet again, soon. I want to be there when they do.

The whole place is overcrowded, and for most people it would be a problem just getting from one end of the room to the other. But not for me, because I'm an old hand at this. It takes years of practice to really be able to slide through a crowd. There's an art to it. It's all about analysis. You have to learn to watch everybody at once, to see which way they're moving, and figure out where the paths will open up. If you're really clever, you can give just one person the slightest bump and make the paths change to what you want.

In a few moments, he'll walk past her table. He'll see her, but she's too busy trying to look busy; she won't see him. He'll walk past her and never see her again.

In two years, he'll still be single. In six years, he'll be married to a woman he hates because he thinks she's his only option. In eighteen years, they'll divorce. It'll be the right choice for them, but not for their son, whose grades will steadily decline. He won't go to university, like he wanted.

In a few moments, she'll be aware that someone is looking at her. She'll let him walk past, without looking up, and she'll never see him again.

In two years, she'll have decided to go back to university and become a teacher. In six years, she'll get a job she likes, teaching English to the smarter kids at a school near her old house. She'll strike up a relationship with Mark – Mr. Harper – who teaches maths. He'll already be married to someone younger and, she imagines, prettier. She'll believe him when he says he's going to divorce her soon. She'll believe it for a long time, and then one day she won't any more, and she'll tell everyone what he is and they'll both be fired. In eighteen years, she'll be living alone in a nice apartment, feel a dull ache in her left side, and nobody will tell her to go to the doctor.

He walks toward her table, now, and she's not going to look up. He sees her, and thinks she looks pretty, even though underneath the table she isn't wearing the shoes he saw. He thinks about saying something to her, but he doesn't. He's no good at that kind of thing, especially when dealing with complete strangers. He's going to pause for maybe half of a second, and then walk away, and they'll never see each other again.

I'm there behind him. I only *need* half a second, I'm not here to do much at all. They don't even notice me. I reach in and put two fingers against the side of her highball glass, half-full of tomato juice and vodka. In that half-second when he's looking at her and she's looking at her phone and neither of them are looking at anything else, I knock the drink into her lap, withdraw my hand and disappear into the crowd.

In one second she'll cry out, and raise both her arms up and away from her lap. in two seconds she'll look up, focus on him, and mistake him for the person who knocked her drink over. In four seconds he'll stammer an apology for something he didn't do. He'll offer to buy her another drink, and to pay for her dry-cleaning. In two hours he'll walk her up to her front door and arrange to see her again, but they won't kiss. Not just yet.

In two years he'll propose to her. He won't have a ring. It won't even be a romantic place. They'll just be walking through town and he'll look over at her, suddenly realise that she's essential and blurt the question out, knowing that if he stops to think about it he might make the wrong choice.

In six years he'll have bought the ring and they'll have saved up enough that they can have a proper wedding. They'll both know that there was never any need to rush things anyway, especially when they had a daughter to take care of.

In eighteen years they'll be living in a pretty little suburban semi. He'll own four suits and three briefcases, and she'll be deputy headmistress of a local comprehensive school. One day she'll feel a dull ache in her left side, and her daughter will insist that she sees a doctor, and it'll be very lucky that they caught it so early.

In fifty-four years, one of them will be there at the end for the other, but it doesn't matter which is which.

That's what I'm good at, see. Analysis. That's how I spotted them in the first place. You look at two people, and you see which way they're moving, and you see where the paths will open up. And if you're really clever, you can give one person the slightest bump and make the paths change to whatever you want.

It's only fifteen seconds later when I leave the club. I glance at the corny bow-and-arrow design on the windows, this time from the inside, and fight the urge to roll my eyes. There are far more elegant ways to do this job. Arrows are for amateurs.

# ESCAPE FROM THE NIGHT TERROR

Emma Scott

"Huh!" Rebecca bolted upright in bed, heart pounding, hands sweating. Something was smothering her. It felt like a bad dream but she was so stifled that it couldn't be. She was tangled, caught up, trapped. She had to escape!

Crashing and tripping down the stairs, she fled - still enfolded in the giant enemy. With a resolute kick, she finally threw it off and reached safety downstairs. There she passed a restless night, huddled in a corner of the kitchen.


The next morning the night terror was fresh in Rebecca's mind. In her bleariness she wondered what she had been struggling with.

"Rebecca?" her father called. "Is there any explanation as to why you're sleeping on the kitchen floor?"

"I had to escape Dad. Something was smothering me."

"This perhaps?" he replied.

Terrified, she turned apprehensively to face her enemy... It was a twisted, beaten-up duvet.

# GOOD GIRL GUIDES

Chrissey Harrison

"You girls have work to do."

The six Girl Guides reluctantly sloped away from the fence that separated our pitch from the neighbouring one where a group of scouts kicked a football about. They walked past me to the QM tent where I was about to set them preparing lunch and one of them, Gemma, shot me a glare.

"You won't be giving me that look when those boys start giving you trouble." I handed her a loaf of bread and some butter.

"We wouldn't mind."

I looked round the group, all of them rolling their eyes in that "Sparrow doesn't know what she's talking about" way. So keen to be adults so soon, but the oldest of them was only thirteen and the youngest was ten.

"Well I know I minded, when I was a Guide."

Mildly curious frowns appeared on a few faces.

"When I was twelve I went on camp to a big scout campsite near Oxford. There were loads of boys there. We thought we knew how to handle them but they were older than us." No one scoffed; I had their interest.

Our group was a small one, only eight Guides and our leaders. Most of us had camped before, on smaller, Guide run sites, but Yewkbury campsite was epic by comparison. We drove past at least a dozen other camps before we reached our site.

Known as the Little Lawn our site was fringed by a tall hedge and we reached it through a pretty little arched gate.

Once we had camp set up, Greenfinch, our head Guider - all our leaders have bird names - gave us free time to go exploring before dinner. We had one goal in mind and that was the shop to get sweets. A little over half way there we met a group of five scouts coming the other way. They stopped and the two older boys slouched against the fence while the three around my age approached us.

"Hey, what's your names?"

I giggled. "Sam."

The other two older girls in our group, Jess and Ella gave their names and then the boys looked to Kelly, who wasn't quite twelve yet.

"None of your business," she said quietly.

Behind her the rest of the group, all ten or eleven years old, kept their eyes on the floor, too shy to say anything.

"I'm Simon, this is Kenny and Tom." He looked over his shoulder at the two older guys, probably both about fifteen or sixteen. "That's Pete and Jason."

Now, the three younger boys were all pretty average looking, kind of scruffy with a smattering of acne, but Jason was pretty swoon worthy; his longer hair tickled his forehead above gorgeous pale blue eyes. Pete was kind of cute too; he wore his t-shirt sleeves rolled up over his shoulders which did funny things to me.

Jess, Ella and I smiled, shyly. "Hi."

A couple of brief smiles flashed across the older boys' faces.

"Where are you camping?" Simon asked.

Jess indicated the way we'd come. "We're on the small Lawn, up that way."

Kelly put her hand on my arm. "Guys, don't. I thought we were going to the shop."

"Oh it's okay, why don't you guys go on, we'll catch up in a bit."

Kelly led the younger girls off down the path while Jess, Ella and I stayed with the boys.

"So, where are you guys camping?" I asked.

"On the beacon field. We're going home the day after tomorrow."

"Shame, we just got here today."

Simon grinned. "Better make the most of it then, come on, we'll show you around." He and his friends took us on a guided tour of the campsite. They showed us the big communal campfire circle, the climbing wall and the assault course. To start with

Jason and Pete hung back but they joined in a bit more when they saw we weren't as immature as boys our age.

We found a rope swing on one of the unoccupied campsites and sat round chatting. Ella climbed up on the swing.

"Hey, I'll push," Simon said, taking up position behind her.

Jess did a couple of handstands and cartwheels, challenging the other boys to see if they could do it too. I sat watching and Pete dropped down on the grass next to me.

"So, how old are you?" he asked.

"Fourteen." My cheeks turned molten and I was sure he knew I was lying. But hey, I was only fourteen months off fourteen, that was nothing really, right?

He smiled. "Cool. I like your hair." He reached out and flicked a dark wavy lock and my molten cheeks went nuclear.

Across the campsite Kelly appeared. She ran over when she spotted us. "You guys. We're supposed to be back at the site! Greenfinch's getting really mad."

I checked my watch as Ella scrambled off the rope swing.

"We've gotta go," I said to Pete.

"That's cool," he said. "How about we meet up later?"

Later? There wasn't much later, was there? "Umm, I don't think so. We might have some free time tomorrow though."

"What, you never snuck out of your tents at night?"

"Er, we really have to go." I grabbed Jess and Ella and followed Kelly back to the campsite.

Greenfinch gave us a lecture about responsibility and trust and how the rules were for our own good, to keep us safe, but what harm was there in talking to a couple of Scouts for a bit? Did it really matter if we were a little late for dinner?

When the sun started to set we gathered around our site's little campfire, toasted marshmallows and sang verse after verse of *Quartermaster's Stores* and *Oh You'll never get to Heaven*. By ten o'clock we were all ready to collapse into bed. Greenfinch sent us down to the toilet block to clean our teeth.

We sang as we walked down, torches bobbing. "Oh you'll never go to heaven."

"On a boyscout's knee."

"Cause a boyscout's knee."

"Is knob-el-y."

A voice from the darkness stunned us into silence. "Hey."

Simon and his friends emerged from behind the toilet block. Pete appeared beside me and a wave of excited butterflies fluttered through me.

"We don't all have knobbly knees you know," he whispered by my ear.

I stifled a giggle.

"You girls wanna come see something cool?" Simon asked.

"We can't," Jess said. "We have to get to bed after we've brushed our teeth."

"But it's only like ten thirty," Pete said.

Simon stepped in front of the door to the toilets, blocking Kelly who was trying to get in. "Yeah, and if we don't let you in you can't brush your teeth so you might as well hang out with us."

"Hey stop it, let me in," Kelly said.

I turned to Pete beside me. "Guys, leave her alone."

He glanced at the younger girls, huddled together behind Ella. "Simon, let 'em go, they're just kids," he said.

"Thanks."

I went to walk past him and he put his hand out to stop me. "I said *they're* just kids. We'll let them go if you and your two friends come see what we have to show you."

I squared my shoulders. "What if I don't care what you want to show me?"

He put his arm around my waist and leaned down to my neck. "Oh I think you'll like it," he whispered. Then he licked my neck and grabbed me round the ass. I shrieked.

"Hey, stop it," Kelly shouted, shoving him in the side. Simon grabbed her by the elbows and held her back.

"Just you then Sammy, you come with me and all your friends can go off to bed like good little Girl Guides."

"Get off me!"

But he was a lot bigger and stronger than me and he backed me up against the wall...

I paused to take the whistling kettle off the stove.

"And? What happened?" Gemma asked.

"What do you think happened?"

She shrugged but her eyes were wide, her mind going to dark places.

"Did he hurt you?"

"Well, you remember I said the younger girls were hanging back? Well a couple of them knew what trouble looked like and went to get Greenfinch. When the boys heard them coming Pete let me go and they all pretended they were just messing around. Greenfinch stood outside while we used the bathrooms to make sure they didn't come back."

Her face sagged with disappointment for a fraction of a second.

"I'd like to say I beat him up and they learned not to mess with Girl Guides but that's not how it works in real life. Truth is if Greenfinch hadn't been there I might have been in serious trouble."

She nodded. "Bet they were scared of Greenfinch."

I smiled. "They may not have learned not to mess with Girl Guides, but they certainly learned not to mess with a Guider!"

# ONE CORPSE TOO MERRY

Christopher M. Geeson

"I know it's home time," DS Reid said at noon, his hands full of tinsel. "But we thought we'd stay around a little longer. Keep you company. We don't like the thought of you working the rest of Christmas Day all on your own, in the office."

"That's a pity," DCI Fraikin replied. 'Spending Christmas Day alone was *exactly* what I had planned. The last thing I want around here is a party.'

But any further discussion was interrupted when the call came through. Before you could say 'twelve drummers drumming' Fraikin and the whole team were heading for the crime scene.

*At least now there's something to wipe the festive grins off their faces*, Fraikin thought, getting out of the car. A package: gift-wrapped in red paper, dotted with white stencilled Santas and green outlines of holly leaves. A package that was five-feet-eight long with two arms, two legs and a head. It was stretched out in the snow-covered alleyway, finished off with a bow of shiny gold ribbon.

Fraikin pulled on his latex gloves and knelt in the snow to touch the gift-wrapped body.

"Dead?" DS Reid asked, hanging back with the rest of the team.

"Stone cold," Fraikin said.

There was a tag bearing a cartoon reindeer's face, hanging from the golden bow. Fraikin flipped it and sighed, his breath hanging like smoke in the cold air. 'That's all I need.'

"What is it, Sir?" Reid asked.

"To DCI Fraikin," he read out loud. 'Merry Christmas, from Saint Nick.' Delivered, no doubt, by some psycho with a grudge against him. Or would this be the first of many gifts left by a new festive serial killer? "Christmas always brings out the best in people, doesn't it, Reid?"

40

"Yes, Sir," said Reid, brushing at some flecks of tinsel still clinging to his jacket.

"Well, better get the damned thing open," Fraikin said. *The sooner we deal with this, the sooner they'll all go home and leave me in peace*, he thought. He undid the bow and began picking at the sticky tape with his gloved fingers. "If I've got to open one present today," he said, turning to Reid and the others, "it might as well be one that puts you off your Christmas dinners."

He took a deep breath and peeled back the tape slowly, starting at the head, waiting for the display of pallid flesh that would follow. Reid and the others gathered around, whispering, like shepherds at the manger. The tape snagged, ripping the paper and exposing the face.

"What the-" Fraikin gasped. The furrowed brow, double chin and protruding bottom lip were all there. He was staring at himself, replicated in smooth, crafted ice. A whole frozen sculpture, made into a perfect scowling copy of him.

"Merry Christmas, Sir," said DS Reid, laughing, 'from all of us on the team.' A squeal of party whistles and loud greetings followed.

Fraikin felt an unwelcome smile tugging at the corners of his mouth. "Reid!" he yelled, getting to his feet. "Just you wait-"

"Why, Sir,' Reid said, 'I do believe you're starting to melt."

## SLUG

Chrissey Harrison

There by a bush on the dimly lit pavement, a dark brown shape. Slender and smooth, it glistens.

As I creep closer the size becomes clear; as long as my foot and fat like a sausage.

The most enormous slug in the world! Then revealed as an elderly, squishy banana.

# HUNGER MOON

Troy Dennison

*This one is for my Uncle Sol who gave me my love for monsters.*

There is a severed arm on top of the television set and I'm reasonably certain that it does not belong to me. For one thing it has a tribal style dragon tattoo coiling around it from the wrist up to the forearm and I have never had a tattoo in my life because I'm terrified of needles. I know that's a terrible thing for a grown man to admit, but I've been scared of them since a horrendous incident with a dentist when I was six years old. I also have a phobia about ducks – but that's another story for another time.

The other reason that I'm fairly sure the arm isn't one of mine is that both of my arms are firmly attached to my body and handcuffed to the large oak dinning room table that I usually eat Sunday lunch at. A rather large nail has been driven through the chain linking the cuffs together and I'm honestly not looking forward to attempting to repair the damage that it has caused to the antique table's waxed surface. No amount of buffing is going to get that particular scar out; I fear that it may require professional attention and that will inevitably cost me a lot of money.

Please don't think that I'm being stingy in any way. Money for me has never really been a concern – I have what you may call inherited wealth – however it grieves me to waste it on anything unnecessary and the damage to the table certainly falls under that particular category. My own arms are stretched out in front of me in a position that requires me to lean uncomfortably across the table; however I feel that complaining about my discomfort would be churlish to say the least, because my limbs are thankfully both still whole. The owner of the tattooed appendage has most certainly not been so fortunate as myself.

A trail of congealed blood from the lone limb has run down the right side of the television screen and made a terrible state of a Persian rug that I had only moved from its long standing home near the hearth two days ago. I am painfully aware from prior experience that no amount of cleaning will fully remove the rust coloured stain that the blood will leave in the rug. Sadly it is as finished as the poor unfortunate whose dragon tattooed arm has led to its current state.

Despite my advancing years my eyesight is still as sharp as it was four decades ago and I can see that the arm bears no sign of being removed by a blade. That would leave a clean wound and the edges of this unfortunate appendage are ragged and uneven. Likewise there are no signs of bite marks, which would be as equally distinctive to identify and this leads me to a singular and unsavoury conclusion - that the limb has been forcibly ripped from its owner's body.

This train of thought continues to another wholly more worrying string of notions; what kind of person could tear someone's arm clean off? Where are they currently? Of more immediate concern is the possibility that they are responsible for my present form of incarceration, which brings me to the final and rather worrying thought that flickers through my mind; what are their intentions towards me?

The cognitive process that I follow to reach this alarming conclusion is hampered mildly by the throbbing sensation that threatens to engulf the back of my head. The pain comes from what I presume to be a rather large contusion that pulses rhythmically to send shivers of eye watering agony through my skull. Someone hit me from behind, rather heavily and to my mind rather unnecessarily; I am, after all, an old man and would appear to pose no obvious physical threat. However, as I struggle to cast my mind back to events earlier this evening, I know with certainty that sometimes appearances can be very, very deceiving.


I watched the sun setting from the French windows that overlook my ornamental herb garden. Glowing embers of orange and gold flickered through the skeletal frames of the trees that border the property some mile and a half distant and I found myself marvelling at the splendid display as I sipped freshly ground Kenyan coffee. I love the majesty of the natural world and it never ceases to surprise and amaze me that the majority of humanity is oblivious to the beauty that surrounds us. I suppose that people are too wrapped up in the minutiae and trivialities that make up their everyday lives to look up for a moment, to gaze past the horizon and let their minds take in the grandeur of our world.

If the weather had been warmer I would have opened the doors and stepped outside, but despite the bright clear day that was ending it was still remarkably cold for late February. My joints ache fiercely when the weather grows cold – which I suppose is only natural considering the years of abuse they have suffered. I led a vigorous and active lifestyle in my youth and, despite my advancing years, I still try to remain as dynamic as ever. A soft tapping at my study door interrupted my reverie and I turned to see Miriam standing in the open doorway. As is customary she was dressed in black, and her auburn hair was pulled back into a severe bun that would have made an elderly school ma'am proud. The broad smile that illuminated her soft, round face was a delightful contrast to her severe appearance.

"We're all ready, sir."

"Very good, my dear. The time seems to have slipped away from me today."

"Will there be anything else?"

"Not this evening Miriam, thank you." I placed the coffee cup on an antique beech table near the French window and followed Miriam as she walked away from my study and down a short corridor to join the rest of the staff. Jacob looked as stone faced as ever, dressed in his usual threadbare clothing which to my mind always gave him the appearance of a taciturn scarecrow. His dress sense was forgiven however because his skill with all things horticultural was without compare.

Shaun stood in stark contrast, bursting with youthful energy in his patterned trousers and chef's blouse, he smiled shyly at me as he spoke "Your dinner's warming in the oven and I've left heating instructions for the weekend meals, sir."

"Thank you, Shaun. I'm sure I shall be fine following them."

"Yes, sir."

My home is no mansion by any stretch of the imagination, however with fifteen rooms it requires constant attention and I have been in the habit of employing a small staff for many years now. Miriam acts as a maid and sometimes secretary for me, I have the taciturn Jacob to maintain the grounds, and my meals are cooked exquisitely by Shaun. My meagre staff all live locally in the village and they depart promptly at four pm each evening. They are always discreet and unobtrusive and I have ample room to house them on the property, but I do enjoy some small measure of solitude; in part because it allows me time to think without fear of disruption. At my age you do a lot of thinking; about the past, the future, regrets and mistakes; it occupies my mind.

Jacob opened the large oak front door and the others followed him outside. Miriam turned and smiled as she left. "Have a good weekend, sir."

"I'm sure I will," I replied, smiling myself. "I shall see you all Monday."

My employees trooped away down the long gravel driveway and I watched them for a moment until the fading light and the cool air of the advancing evening drove me back inside. I turned the key in the lock and sighed softly to myself, taking in the vast blanket of silence that always seems to descend when I am alone.

I met the girl of my dreams many years ago; her name was Victoria and she was the one great love of my life; as beautiful as the dawn and as passionate as the fiery sun itself. We were perfect for each other and I would have happily spent every waking hour with her until the end of my days but we were only together for a short time before fate tore her from me.

Cancer; that dreadful disease is still as feared and reviled today as it was back then. One moment I had everything to live for, a future that was full of bright promise and the next... nothing, just a hollow emptiness in my heart where once there had been joy and boundless love. There was never anyone else after Victoria; no one made me feel the way she did and to my mind nobody ever came close to filling the void she left in my life. I have been so terribly alone for such a very long time now.

For several days each month at irregular intervals the staff are not required to work. Sometimes I am away on business trips and at others I am here alone. This particularly cold weekend in February was one of the latter occasions. My big plans for the weekend revolved around eating some of Shaun's delicious meals and finally coming to grips with the latest Cussler bestseller. I do so like his writing; full of thrilling exploits of adventure revolving around the ocean and its mysteries.

My library is well stocked; I have a literary preference for thrillers and historical novels and for the most part I abhor the horror genre and steer clear of its lurid authors. I do like Stephen King however, and I find his skill at weaving a gripping story peopled with fascinating characters to be most satisfying. I do enjoy a nice glass of wine with my reading and, to that end I keep a small but well stocked selection of bottles.

Many years ago now an inquisitive maid entered the wine cellar, saw the array of hooks and chains mounted to the walls and ceiling beams and jumped to the erroneous conclusion that I had a predilection towards fetishism and BDSM. I suppose I could have truthfully claimed that the house's previous owner placed them there, but as the previous owner was my father I chose to remain silent on the subject. I also placed a rather heavy lock on the cellar door and hid the key, inevitably however, rumours concerning my sexual orientation and interests surfaced.

I know there has been a great deal of idle speculation locally as to why I spend so much time by myself in this big old empty house. Rumour and gossip have been rife for decades and I am sure that I have been the subject of an endless parade of conjecture over the years. The one most favoured is that I am gay, something that never fails to bring a smile to my face. I suppose that theory was not helped when I hired young Shaun, and I am more than a little relieved that my employees do not live with me.

Poor Shaun is nowhere nearly as thick skinned as I am and for his sake more than for my own I am glad that I have not provided more fuel to that particular fire. His skill as a chef is unquestionable and I look forward to each meal with delight; this evening my repast was to be one of his specialities, something of the Italian persuasion. With that thought firmly in mind I turned and began to walk towards my kitchen.

After cautiously donning oven gloves to remove my dinner from the oven I was not disappointed to discover that this evenings meal was to be one of Shaun's lasagne verdi recipes.

Layers of ricotta, parmesan and mozzarella cheese sandwiched between the green pasta and sauce and topped off with a delicate three cheese sauce. I chose to accompany the meal with a glass of rather nice eighty-two Chianti, which I have always found goes well with any tomato based dish.

I ate at the large counter that stands in the centre of my kitchen, enjoying the latent warmth from the oven and the delightful taste of my food. After I had finished I loaded the dish, cutlery and glass into the dishwasher and slowly made my way back towards the front of the house. The night was still young and I decided to read in my study with some music playing softly in the background; perhaps jazz.

I have always loved jazz; the shifting flow of the music, as constantly changing as the tides of the sea or the phases of the moon as it transforms with each note, becoming something new and unexpected. My favourite was the great showman Cab Calloway, who was a wonderful singer and dancer. Minnie the Moocher is still one of my favourite songs and I can still recall the thrill I felt when I heard it for the first time so many years ago now. His career spanned more than six decades yet he's only remembered for that one song; and perhaps his appearance in the Blues Brothers. Still, I suppose it's better to be remembered for something than to slip away from this life unnoticed.

Now there was a gloomy thought and far from what I wanted to have on my mind through the long weekend that beckoned. In truth I have tried to live my own life in relative obscurity and if at some future point I slip from this existence with barely a murmur of notice then I shall die a happy man. I have never sought attention or celebrity and regard myself as a thoroughly uninteresting individual; hence my need for the excitement of Cussler's heroes. My thoughts threatened to turn towards an unwholesome introspection, but it was at that precise moment that I heard the frantic knocking at the front door.

I paused mid-step and turned back; perhaps one of the staff had forgotten something. Miriam had left her handbag on more than one occasion and so I was unconcerned as the frenzied knocking came again. I reached the door, unlocked it and opened it a fraction to cautiously to peer out because I have no security chain or peep hole.

The girl was exquisitely beautiful in a waifish way but the look of terror on her face and the fear in her eyes as they locked onto mine marred her striking looks at that moment. "Please."

"What is it, my dear?"

"Please! You have to help me." Her eyes darted around like startled butterflies as the girl spoke. "My car broke down. There was a man, he stopped. I thought he was trying to help me but..."

"Calm yourself."

"I got away, ran away, and then I saw the light in your window. Help me? Please?"

I struggled for a moment before answering, torn by doing the right thing and maintaining the peace and quiet that I so desperately craved. The girl sobbed and against my better judgement I heard myself say, "Yes of course, I can call the police for you."

In the instant that I said those words the girl let out a piercing shriek of terror. While I had been focused on her face she had turned to look back down my driveway and saw something in the darkness that had prompted her cry. If the girl was beautiful then the man, in complete contrast, was the most unattractive I have ever seen. His face was made up of angles and planes, framed by broad, Slavic cheekbones, and an aquiline nose. His eyes were dark and piercing even in the lengthening twilight and he ran towards us with a purposeful stride that ate up the distance to the house. The girl screamed again and I found myself reacting without thinking.

I reached for her arm and shouted, "inside, now!" The girl almost flew over the threshold and past me into the house. In those scant seconds the man had reached the steps to the house and, as I slammed the door and turned the key, I felt the old oak shake as the man hammered into it. The door reverberated as he rained a flurry of angry blows into the wood and the sound of each one echoed like distant thunder through the house.

My mind was racing; this was not good, this was not good at all. I had to do something to get the girl to safety and remove the maniac from my front step. I had to call the police immediately and they would be able to sort this out with a minimum of fuss. The man had stopped banging on the door and a harsh silence had descended. I was about to take advantage of the momentary respite to call for assistance and began to turn from the door, and it was then that the girl hit me over the head and the world turned a crushing black.

I should be scared; I should be losing my mind after finding myself in this predicament. I should, but I am calm, I am curious and I know full well that if I succumb to panic it will only attract the attention of whoever has me incarcerated. That meeting is something I have no wish to hasten, especially if their treatment of the owner of the unfortunate arm is any gauge of their intentions.

I am painfully aware of the severed limb and despite trying not to think about it I find my attention drawn back again and again. I fancy that I can smell the decomposition setting in; that sweet, foetid aroma that accompanies rotting flesh. Does the air have the faintest coppery taint from the blood? I am sure that I am imagining far too much, letting my fancy run away with itself rather than focusing on my present dilemma.

I have no way of noting the passing of time as I choose not to wear a watch, so I have no idea how long I have been unconscious. The chair to which I find myself currently confined sits facing a large window. During the day you can see clear across to the small river that crosses my property half a mile away. It currently looks like a wall of black ice and the only thing I can see in the window is my own reflection; I look old.

If the lights in the room were turned out I would be able to see clearly through the window. Tonight is a full moon and I could easily see it and roughly gauge the amount of time that I have been incarcerated. Instead I have my own sad reflection to stare at; anything is preferable to the appendage adorning my television.

I do not actually watch the television, and I would certainly never stoop to crassly viewing it while eating; it is here because there was nowhere else for it. I own it because it seemed that everyone owns one these days, but I never liked it in any of the other rooms and now at least I have a reason to get rid of the infernal device if I survive whatever it is that is currently happening to me.

"I see that our host is back with us."

I jump slightly at the sound of the deep voice from the doorway and I turn towards it with a sick feeling in my stomach. I can see the man from my driveway earlier standing there regarding me coldly. The man moves with a sinuous grace that belied his size; it almost seems that he glides as he enters the room and the power in his gaze is soul shattering. The last time I saw a creature move that way was in the sweltering heat of the Burmese jungle many years ago.

The tiger had barely acknowledged my presence as he slid through the dense greenery; and for that I was eternally grateful. The man in front of me now has the same predatory quality to his character; the unquestionable knowledge that he is at the top of the food chain and you are being casually regarded as a potential meal. This particularly unsavoury thought is given emphasis by the faint traces of blood around the man's cruel lips and grained into his fingernails.

"I will ask questions, you will provide answers. Do you understand?" His voice is deep, but with an underlying melodic quality and the faintest hint of an accent; mid-European perhaps? I nod slightly and lower my eyes to the tabletop; I have no wish to gaze on his cruel face if I can help it.

"You live alone here?"

"Yes." I am shocked to hear how steady my voice is, almost confident and without the faintest tremor to my words.

"Visitors?"

"No one is expected, and my staff are away now until Monday."

"Good, very good. You are of course telling me the truth?"

"Yes, absolutely."

"I would hate to think that you were lying. I do not like liars and I do not like unexpected guests."

"I can assure you that it is the truth."

"I hope so. For your sake."

The implied threat in his words is not wasted on me and I find my eyes flickering towards the television and its grotesque decoration. The man must have seen me look because his next words chill me to the core.

"Just a little snack Carina bought along in case we were peckish."

I look up sharply and the man laughs; a deep rolling roar that makes the hairs on the back of my neck stand up. A snack? He can't be serious can he? That is patently ridiculous. I can see the man as a burglar, obviously and a killer possibly, but a cannibal? That was stupid, insane even. People, in my experience, simply do not go around eating other people. Killing them, yes, but eating them, never. He is obviously trying to get a reaction from me, make me more unnerved and afraid than I already am. That is surely his intent, and it is working.

The man turns and looks out of the window for a moment, studying his own reflection in the glass before he draws the curtains and shuts out the night. He pulls a chair out from under the table and drapes himself on it casually. It almost feels as if I can sense the raw power that the man exudes. The intensity and sheer indomitable will rolls off him in a wave. Again I am reminded of my encounter with the tiger and the same sharp fear that had been inside me so many years ago returns with a dreadful clarity.

There is something unsettling about the man, something in his voice and the way he seems to flow like water when he moves; it is disquieting and it strikes some deep primal chord inside me. He scares me, although perhaps scares is too strong a word to use. His presence certainly makes me uncomfortable and there is something about his mouth; not an overbite but some similar peculiarity or distortion of his teeth that disturbs me greatly.

"Look what I found." The girl enters the room waving a pair of glasses and a bottle of wine in her hands. "He has a cellar full."

"Excellent," the man responds.

The girl pours a glass and offers it to the man; he sniffs it gently and then sips appreciatively. From the faint smell I can tell that it is a bottle of Bordeaux, probably the eighty-three; they have good taste in my wine. Carina is even more beautiful now that I have time to look at her properly, but it is a pale, ethereal beauty. Her skin has a faintly translucent quality so that it gives her an almost magical aura; as if she were some strange creature from the realm of faerie.

"That's not the only thing he had in his cellar."

"Go on?"

The girl flicks a glance at me and the look of malevolence, lasciviousness and sheer wanton lust that she directs towards me is stomach turning.

"Hooks, chains; it's a perverts paradise down there."

"It seems that there's more to our host than meets the eye." The man raises an enquiring eyebrow in my direction.

"I can't imagine him getting up to much, he looks past it. Can you see him wearing rubber from head to toe? Spiked mask, zipper for a mouth, getting himself off watching the vicar shagging an Alsatian?"

"You do have an imagination, Carina."

"He's rich, he lives alone, I bet he sends his staff away so he can have massive orgies. Places like this are a nest of repressed sexual frustration and forbidden vices where anyone can indulge themselves in anything if they've got the money for it."

"Shocking." The smile on his face gives the impression that the man's shock is merely being paid lip service.

"Whips and chains and handcuffs and leather. First it's willing partners and then maybe some that are less than willing, that need a little persuasion, and after that it's just a step away from kiddie porn and mail order Philippino school boys!"

"You've heard the charges laid against you, how do you plead?" The man leers at me from across the table.

"Plead? I don't understand." I manage to stammer out the words, but the girls vitriolic outburst has shaken me.

"To Carina's charges. Are you some strange, rich fetish-freak?"

"God no! Of course not."

"So why do you have all those chains in your cellar?" the girl asks.

"My father put them there a long time ago." I can scarcely believe that even under my present circumstances I find it difficult to talk about my father's modifications in the cellar.

"Were you a bad boy? Did he chain you up and beat you or did he abuse you in other ways?" Her face gleams with curiosity and then a mocking look enters her eyes as she lowers her voice and says "Come down to the cellar son, Daddy has something to show you."

"No! It was nothing like that at all."

"There's a shame." Her face falls and she seems visibly crushed for a moment, but then the gleam enters her eyes again as she runs a finger down the man's neck and says, "we could always go down and play with them later lover, it's a shame to see them go to waste."

I have noticed the same peculiarities about the girl that the man possessed. Her movements are graceful like a ballet dancer, and the same feral look of raw power is etched on her face. Even her mouth reminds me of his; perhaps they share the same edge of cruelty to their smiles or their corrupting nature is slipping through the thin veneer of humanity that they outwardly display. Then again it could be down to the way her eyes keep straying to my neck and her tongue moistens her lips as if in anticipation.

"Why are you here?" I pluck up the courage to ask.

The man pauses before answering, regarding me thoughtfully with his dark, brooding eyes. "I saw the lights, they looked warm and inviting and I have no desire to spend another cold night outdoors. We expected people, some sport and sustenance." He smiles at the thought and his teeth glitter. "Instead we find one little old man rattling around this big empty house like a penny in a coffee jar."

"Well I'm sorry to be such a disappointment to you."

The girl sniffs in disdain. "He smells old. You know I like my food fresher."

"Patience my sweet, there will be others soon."

"I want the maid; I've never feasted on a maid before. A maid for breakfast." She smiles at the distasteful thought and then turns to me again, "Does your maid give you a special 'breakfast' every morning? Does she take your wrinkled, old, disease-ridden cock in her mouth and pretend it's the best she's ever had? Does she?" Carina's voice begins to raise in anger. "Oh master you're the only one for me, you're so big and hard and I could just suck you all day long! Bastard!"

As she screams Carina pitches the half empty bottle of wine past my head. It comes so close to hitting me that I feel the wind as it passes and explodes against the wall. I sit rigid in my chair, desperate to run, to flee from these mad people before they hurt me or worse.

"Carina, I was enjoying that."

"Sorry. It was his fault." The girl casts me the most evil look I've ever seen on a living creature.

"Perhaps another bottle?" The man sighs softly as he speaks.

The girl glares at him for a moment and then she grasps a handful of his hair, draws his head back and kisses him in the most wanton display of intimacy I have ever had the misfortune to witness. They part at last, gasping for breath, finished with each other for the moment, and for that small mercy I am grateful.

"Don't start having fun without me," the girl says, and casts me an evil wink as she heads towards the door.

I watch her as she leaves and it is only when she is gone that I realise how tense my body has become; on edge, taught as a bow string, ready to snap at any moment. The man must notice my distress because he says, "not to worry, Carina is well fed and she can wait until your staff arrive for her entertainment."

If the words are meant to make me feel less nervous then they fail and I shudder inwardly at the thought of that inhuman individual getting her hands on Miriam or poor Shaun. What sort of sick, twisted creatures are they? The word seemed to fit all too well because the pair barely seemed human at all to my eyes.

The man sips from his glass and says, "I never drink wine."

"I'm sorry?"

"Nothing, a personal amusement." A wry smile plays on his face as he speaks. "Why do you live here alone?"

"I like it that way; I enjoy the quiet."

"Too much time alone is bad for you, wallowing in the thoughts that wrap themselves through your mind like a nest of vipers. Sometimes you need people around you. You need to feel the pulse of life, the warm throbbing of humanity's vitality; so hot and rich and thick that it could choke you if you let it, but oh so sweet to savour."

I must look truly alarmed at his words because the man begins to laugh. My wrists are beginning to chafe on the handcuffs and a deep ache has set into my muscles. I have been sitting too long, chained to the table and I can feel the beginning of a mild headache; a stiffening in my neck, and a faint throb in my forehead that his laughter was not helping one bit. A faint sheen of sweat stands out from my brow and I fancy that my heart is beating faster, echoing like some loud kettle drum. I am sure the man can hear it because his eyes narrow for a moment.

"Are you ill? Are you dying?"

"It's nothing, not life threatening at least. I suffer from a particular ailment, a hereditary genetic condition that causes me some discomfort from time to time."

"Are you contagious?"

"Good heavens no, it's more of a...well it's like being allergic to nuts or lactose intolerant. You make adjustments, change your lifestyle in a way that will accommodate your illness and then you carry on living."

"So this illness is under control?"

"Oh yes, completely."

"Are you required to take medication?"

"No, don't worry."

"Good." He sits in silence for a long moment and then says, "I think I understand what you mean; changing your lifestyle to accommodate something that has happened to your body. How intriguing that we should have something in common other than age."

"Age? You're thirty if you are a day."

"No, I am far, far older than that."

"Really?"

"Really. I am so much older than my looks. I have lived for a long, long time and I have seen things, done things that most men could not even dream of. I am much older and perhaps a little wiser than I was in my youth and I have learned many harsh lessons. The hardest thing in life is to outlive your loved ones, to watch them wither and die and become dust in the wind. Seeing your friends growing old and frail while you still feel the same inside as you did years ago, watching your children dying; these things can break a man's heart and tear out his soul."

I can hear the truth in his words, and in all honesty it is something that I know the pain of myself. First Victoria, then my father; one by one over the years the nearest and dearest in my life have faded and passed. I feel the hollow pain in my chest as the memories stir. There are moments when I wish I could turn back time and return to the days when life was good, when Victoria was alive and I was in love, back before everything changed. I may wish, but I know that it will never happen; the past is the past, long gone except for the bitter sweet memories.

"That sounds like a rather lonely existence."

"So says the man who chooses to live alone."

"There was little choice involved, I never married and I never had children because I could not bear to see them go through what I have had to endure."

"Your illness?"

"Yes. "

"A lonely existence indeed."

"It could have been, I don't really see it that way."

"Would you change things if you could? Go back to the beginning and take a different path?"

"To live my life again? It's crossed my mind over the years, but am I tempted if such a thing were possible? No, one lifetime is enough for me."

"There is never truly enough time to live and youth is wasted on the young."

The man drains his glass and stands up, regarding me again with those dark, dreadful eyes before walking to the door. He pauses at the thresholds and says, "I shall leave you for a while, but rest assured I shall return and we can talk some more."

"I shall be waiting right here." I reply, with a barely disguised irony.

The man laughs as he turns to leave and, in the moment before he flips off the light switch and plunges the room into darkness, I see what had been eluding me. His canine teeth appear to be...no, that cannot be right, my eyes must be deceiving me. It is the light, or my nerves, that is all. There is no way that he could possibly have fangs. Is there?

The door closes with a harsh finality and my mind races as I sit alone in the dark. Could such things really exist? If they are real, then what do I know about them? All my information comes from fiction, from books and films and how reliable can that be? I know that most of modern werewolf lore comes directly from The Wolfman movie featuring Lon Chaney all those years ago now. Zombies are all that Romero chap's doing, so who is to say what is real or fiction when it comes to people like these.

It is something to consider, no matter how wildly incredulous such thoughts are. I need to occupy my mind as I sit here in the darkness and I have no wish to think further about my possible fate at the hands of this pair of insane people. There has to be a way to focus myself, to look past the ache in my muscles, the pain in my joints. This is when I realise that I can actually see the room. There is a light source somewhere and after a moment I see it; a faint beam of light touching the table's surface in front of me.

My eyes are drawn upwards and I can see the cause of the soft illumination; a gap in the curtains. Moonlight is cascading through the window, casting a pale, spectral glow into the room. If I lean to my right somewhat it is possible that I could see the full moon outside and gauge the length of my imprisonment. Luck is with me and the moon lines up perfectly with the gap in the curtains. It hangs there in the night sky, big and bright and almost welcoming in its familiarity. At a glance I knew that it is roughly seven pm, and that my unconscious state and imprisonment have only lasted a short time. The night is young, the moon is full and the evening stretches out ahead of me

Each phase of the full moon has several names; February is known as the Snow Moon or Hunger Moon. Now there is an appropriate name if I ever heard one. I've always felt that Hunger Moon has an unsettling note to it. To my mind it sounds too much like some sort of wild appetite or need, as if there was some underlying desperate menace to the name. I have seen that frantic desire in the eyes of my captors and it fills me with a cold dread to the very core of my being.

There is another name for the February full moon however, an older and much more appropriate name to which I feel a particular kinship; Wolf Moon. A true full moon lasts for mere moments, but it can appear full to the naked eye for several days. The effects of the full moon however last much longer.

The joints in my fingers are aching now, and not just from the mild arthritis which has plagued me for many years. I focus on my hands, the shape, the symmetry, I see the small scar that came from a childhood accident, so old, so familiar and yet still strongly carved in my flesh after all this time. I look at the handcuffs and the damaged table surface and then my eyes are drawn to the door; such a shame that it has been shut.

A shiver runs through me and the chain on the handcuffs rattles against the nail that holds it secure. The sound is harsh and rasping in the silence that enfolds me and I fancy that I can hear my own breathing, noisy and panting, my heart thumping louder and louder in my chest. A second shudder passes through me and this time I almost gasp aloud in shock.

As I kick my shoes off I recall the strange conversation that I have just had. Every one of my answers was truthful, but there is quite a stretch between telling the truth and telling the whole story. I live alone in part by choice and in part because of my affliction, and while it is true that my father installed the chains in the cellar I have found occasion to use them myself in the past. I wager that the use I put them to would surprise my unpleasant visitors no end.

The pain in my muscles is a dull ache now and it burns like a fire through my body. I close my eyes for a moment and when I open them I can the see the hair on the back of my arms as it lengthens, thickens and becomes dark and coarse. Another stab of pain courses through me and as I clench my fists against it my nails draw deep groves into the surface of the table. I almost feel sorry for the furniture as I deface it further; I fear that it may be beyond repair after this abuse.

I find myself laughing softly but the laughter turns from a low growl at the back of my throat to a snarl. I spare a last fleeting thought for my unwanted guests, but they hold no sympathy in my heart. They are thieves and killers and if there is a shred of humanity in either of them it is submerged deep beneath their inhuman appetites. They have killed tonight and perhaps many times before, so perhaps this is justice of a kind; the justice of tooth and claw, of blood and bone.

The light of the full moon washes over me and as another wave of pain runs its course I hunch forwards and the air is filled with the sound of my vertebrae cracking and popping as they shift and change shape. I flex my arms and the handcuffs come apart, the links of the chain falling like demented confetti onto the table, glittering in the moonlight; the Hunger Moon, the Wolf's Moon.

I live alone because it is necessary, I live alone because I am cursed, or perhaps blessed. I stand apart from the rest of the world and watch as it drifts by, padding silently through the night on velvet paws. I am at one with my nature and the world around me, every single fibre of my being infused with the power of the predator, the hunter, the wolf inside.

I taste blood in my mouth as my teeth elongate and then I feel my jaw changing shape to accommodate the new incisors and canines that thrust themselves through my gums. Is it any wonder that I loath dentists? There is a perceptible shift in my vision as some of the colours drain away, but the lack of colour is balanced by an increase in clarity as my senses become magnified. I can smell the severed arm decomposing, rotting slowly and my mouth waters in anticipation. There is prey nearby and as I give myself up to the change the wolf comes to ascendancy and I lift my muzzle high and let out a howl that rips the night apart.

And then I begin to hunt.

# SPACE:
# A REMORSELESS CALCULATED
# INEXACTITUDE

John H. Barnes


When I first travelled to this planet boredom of past led me on,
Seeking to walk on this world, I kept my body from the sun,
I wanted my solar battery to remain empty, all my power gone,
Though life is out there, days of travel in nothing isn't fun.

The only interests to see, were a galaxy here and a galaxy there,
Some planets hold life, some do not, but they seek company,
And boredom isn't lonely, it is here, it is there, it is every where,
I watched through prisms of glass, as my home became history.

Two days have gone, the world where I was, I could see no more,
Just the lifeless miles where no anger, love or hatred will be,
Life in a neutral cold, seeing nothing to comfort a heart that's
    sore,
And in ten thousand years I will see my tomorrows' destiny.

Taking the hope that in time new life forms might walk with me,
Until then I look and see the black, a void devoid of reality.
In this emptiness, where dreams are made then go for you to see,
To find a home, a corner in the endless, unending infinity.

On the third day I tried to think what work I could have done,
Calling out, asking what will be, asking the dark what was.
Its reply was the cold undead loving hatred of senses not won,
A remorseless calculated inexactitude of a living carcass.

## SPACE...

From the spacecraft I'd stare to a globe I'd soon know as home,
A growing speck of light on the horizon of a darkened ball,
Securing a might from the mists that shroud the doubled dome,
Closer 'til colours breached the mist like a crocheted shawl.

My craft secured on the dark side of the moon on this fourth day,
That flight now over, journey to the earth for flora and fauna,
Sending back reports of the natural resources that I can convey,
Understanding the flowers and animals, not being a mourner.

*The term calculated inexactitude was favoured by Winston Churchill. As, when in the houses of parliament it was considered bad form to refer to another politician as a liar, so he would say, 'they just said a calculated inexactitude'.*

# THE REAL EVIL

Chrissey Harrison

"You know goblins live in the churchyard, right?" Liam teased his little sister, Sarah.

"Nu-uh, you're making that up." She kicked a bunch of leaves at him and he froze.

"Oh, you are dead."

He stooped, scraped together a handful of crisp brown leaves and chased after her. She bolted along the path through the church garden, shrieking.

A dark, hooded figure appeared in front of her and she skidded to a halt. Liam's handful of leaves hit her square in the back and exploded into a fluttering cloud. The figure in front of them grunted and raised a withered hand towards Sarah.

Liam snagged her arm. "Run!"

Everyone said monsters lived in the churchyard, but Liam never expected to see a real live one! The sun hovered just above the horizon, casting its last golden light over everything. At this time of day all the ghosts and goblins could be creeping from their hiding places.

"Come on Sarah, run! We have to get to hallowed ground. The graveyard, quick!"

They rounded the back corner of the church, but Sarah tripped on one of the spreading roots of the churchyard yew tree. Liam stopped, pulled her up into his arms and dragged her to the wall of the church. With their backs pressed to the sun warmed stone, they listened for any sound that the creature was following them.

"Shh."

Instead of shuffling footsteps or guttural moans, they heard the soft sounds of a woman singing. Her high, sweet voice carried from the graveyard at the far end of the church.

Liam turned to Sarah and put his finger across his lips. She nodded and they crept silently along the wall. When they reached the corner, they peered round; Sarah poked her head out below his.

A young woman sat beside a grave, her pure white dress draped across the floor like a shimmering puddle. Even though only a slight breeze stirred the air, her hair flowed out beside her.

"Look," Sarah whispered.

The beautiful sound of the woman's voice abruptly ceased and Liam froze. She lifted her head and slowly turned to face them.

"Come closer, children," she called, in a voice like ringing silver bells. She rose to her feet and held her hands out for them.

Liam and Sarah stepped cautiously out from behind the wall. The low sun, setting now behind the woman, cast its rays through the hazy Autumn air and made it look like she was glowing.

"Come closer."

They slowly moved towards her and she smiled. Liam had never seen such a radiant smile.

Sarah hurried towards the angelic woman, but Liam was content to bask in her light as he took small steps across the grass.

The sound of heavy footsteps and panting breaths behind them briefly shattered the wonderful moment. Liam glanced over his shoulder to see the dark, shambling figure from before. It leaned on the wall, gasping for breath, its shrivelled hand clutched to its chest.

"Get, away, from them," it wheezed.

Sarah screamed and Liam's head snapped back round. The enchanting vision vanished and in her place floated a mass of black rags and twisted thorns, with one taloned hand clasped around his sister's wrist. The air turned chilly and raised goosebumps all up his arms.

"Come with me, children," the twisted creature cackled. "You have such shiny, pretty souls."

"No, leave her alone!" Liam darted forward and tried to claw the creature's hand from Sarah's arm, but her grip was hard as iron. Sarah's skin turned white from the pressure and she whimpered. Tears gathered in her eyes.

Then something sailed through the air and hit the creature square in the face. Her grip loosened and Liam prised her fingers away. Sarah dropped to the ground, free. The mystery object that saved them lay on the grass and revealed itself to be a garden trowel.

They scrambled back and the beast with the crippled hand moved in front of them, holding something up towards the creature.

"Begone, leave this place!"

Liam stared at its feet. Under the ragged overcoat it wore jeans and workman's boots.

The black rag woman hissed and screeched. Liam and Sarah clamped their hands over their ears.

"This is a sacred place, you have no power here, begone she-devil. I banish you. Begone!"

With an earsplitting wail that Liam could feel in his stomach, the devil woman spun into a blur, which contracted into a point before vanishing with a flash of green light.

"You kids shouldn't be here. Don't you know it's dangerous at night?" The man tucked his Bible back into his overcoat, turned to them and lowered his hood.

"I know you," Liam said, getting to his feet. "You're Mr Hawthorne, the gardener."

Mr Hawthorne tutted and reached out his good hand to help a trembling Sarah to her feet.

"Thank you, for saving us." Liam said. "How did you know what to do?" He picked up the fallen trowel and handed it back to its owner.

"I was a preacher once, before the devil took an interest in me." Mr Hawthorne held up his withered hand in evidence. "I never stopped believing, but I couldn't preach about evil being this invisible force in our lives when I knew different. People don't want to hear sermons about goblins and ghouls."

He shepherded them to the church gate.

"Now, you kids run along home."

Sarah scurried down to the pavement but Liam paused. "Wait, Mr Hawthorne, sir. Can you teach me how to fight monsters?"

The old man smiled. "We'll see lad."

# DYING TO BE PETTED

Chrissey Harrison

We swim, we eat. There's not much more to being a goldfish.

Outside the tank we see the humans stroking their pet dog. When those warm blooded hands dip into the tank to clean the glass, we brush against them and wish that, just once, we could be petted too.

# WORST VALENTINE'S NIGHT EVER

Jim Cogan

*I'm dreading this, literally, with my recent luck this is certain to go badly,* he thought as he nervously crossed the floor of the crowded bar, searching for the lady with the red carnation. And, there she was, sat alone at the very first table near the front door, where she could survey everyone entering the bar. As he approached he observed the half full wine glass in one hand, and there in the other hand, the now slightly bedraggled looking red carnation. No doubt it had looked bright and fresh at the start of the evening, but as time had worn on she had obviously taken to handling it a little too much. *Probably down to anxiety,* he thought to himself. *Oh well, here goes...*

*This has been such a disaster, I knew, absolutely one hundred percent knew, that this was going to be a terrible idea,* thought Zara, the lady with the red carnation. *Why, oh why did I ever agree to this, what madness lead me to go along with it? Me, going on a blind date, a bloody blind date – I'm thirty two, for goodness sake, this is the kind of stuff you do in your early twenties! And on Valentine's Night. What a gullible idiot I am. How did I ever let him convince me? Stupid internet dating!*

Zara glanced at her watch, then confirmed the time on clock on the wall behind the bar, then cursed herself for doing that. *Sily girl,* she thought, *you've been doing that every five minutes since you arrived, if you keep it up then people will start to notice. Damn it, where is he?*

*I'm the girl, I'm the one allowed to be late – not too late, fashionably late – about five minutes or so, no more. Not the guy, he is absolutely not allowed to be late, he's supposed to be fashionably early, then he's allowed to get a little nervous as the agreed time passes, then he's supposed to be relieved as I arrive, fashionably late, that's how it's supposed to happen.* Zara cursed herself for being guilty of breaking this rule herself – she'd never been any good at judging the whole fashionably late thing. She'd set off in good time to beat the traffic, only on that night there was very little and she'd got to the bar about ten minutes early. For a brief moment she thought about walking straight past the door of the bar and doing another lap around the block to pass the time, but it was a bit chilly out, and her choice of heels didn't really lend themselves to walking in anything more than short bursts. And she was thirty-two, a grown woman, for goodness sake, she didn't have to pander to these stupid rules now, did she? Well, he'd arranged to meet her at eight pm, she'd been there since ten to – and he was now officially forty-five minutes late.

"I know," he'd suggested in an email. "Lets not exchange photos before we meet, why don't we challenge the modern obsession of making advance judgements on purely visual perception – why don't we just meet up for a date and see what happens? And hey, its Valentine's night this Saturday, its audacious, but why not? Why shouldn't Valentine's night be good for a first date and not just for couples in established relationships?"

"But how will find each other if we don't know what the other looks like?" she'd asked.

"Wear a red carnation," he'd replied.

It had seemed quite romantic at the time.

*All of those things would cause alarm bells to ring for anyone else – but me – no. I've bloody gone along with it, like a complete fool, against all my better instincts, and surprise surprise, he's not bleeding turned up!*

"Um, hi, excuse me, would you happen to be Zara?"

The voice coming from behind her suddenly wrenched her out of her mental rant. *Oh my God, its him! He's finally arrived! I don't know whether to be angry that he's left me waiting for so long or glad that he's actually made it!* Her mind was suddenly a hazy clutter – this was the moment of truth, she stood up slowly and began to turn around to face the owner of the voice.

*Oh wow, he's actually quite cute, slightly younger than I was expecting, not disgracefully so, mind you, but I'd bet he's younger than me. And he's pretty good looking, makes you wonder why he was so reluctant to show me his photo, I doubt many girls would find his physical appearance anything less than pleasant. Oh well, better say something I guess.*

"Yes, that's me, and you must be Mick," she said in what she hoped was an endearing tone of voice, she moved to extend her hand towards him in a welcoming gesture. "It's lovely to finally meet you–" She was so caught up in the moment that she'd forgotten about the half full glass of wine in her hand. *Oh my god, Zara, what have you done! You are such a clumsy idiot.* "Oh, oh dear, I'm really sorry about that."

He stood there before her, a sizable and very visible damp patch slowly spreading across the front of his shirt.

*Curious*, she thought, *he almost looks like he was expecting that. And anyway, he turned up forty five minutes late, he should be damn grateful I chose not to simply tip my drink all over his head!*

"It's okay, it's not that bad, just a small spillage – and minor soaking – I'll survive."

"I'm so sorry, Mick, I'm all thumbs, but it's okay – it's a mild white wine, that should come out in the wash no problem. Be thankful I don't drink red!" *Good recovery, and nice little ice-breaker joke at the end there, go girl, you can turn this around.*

"Yes, that's very true. But anyway, look, Zara, you've got this wrong, I'm not actually Mick."

"Excuse me?" *Okay, this is weird, what gives?*

"I'm Peter, I work here, behind the bar."

"Ah." *Oh no, Zara you complete idiot, he's just the barman.* It was true, she hadn't been paying attention earlier as she was very nervous about the date, but now she could recall that it was in fact Peter who had served her that very drink that she had now accidentally poured over him.

"Look, you're probably not going to like what I'm about to say, but I think it might be easier if I just tell you straight. Mick rang through to the bar and left a message for you, he says he's sorry, but he's had second thoughts about the whole thing and decided it wasn't such a good idea after all. He'll send you an email to explain, but he won't be turning up tonight."

"Right," said Zara, slowly deflating like a party balloon leaking air.

"And he's sorry he left you waiting for so long before phoning."

"Okay." *Bastard.*

"What can I say? I'm sorry."

"No, it's okay, it's not your fault. Shouldn't shoot the messenger, and all that. And, again, I'm so sorry about your shirt."

"It's fine, don't mention it, happens all the time."

"Um, Peter. I think it's about time I had another drink."


An hour later the bar was almost empty, most of the regulars apparently out having Valentine's meals with their partners. Zara had relocated herself to a comfortable stool by the bar, where upon Peter kept her supplied with drinks while she endeavoured to explain the circumstances that had led her there.

"I can't believe you agreed to it. He seriously wouldn't even show you a photo?"

"I know, it was stupid, but you know what - for all the worries I had, like was he some kind of bunny boiling psycho or an axe murderer, or a date rapist or something, I'm actually pretty hacked off that I didn't even get to find out. Oh well, that's the sorry story of my evening, bet you can't top that?"

"Well, actually. This morning I had a girlfriend, and this evening I had a romantic Valentine's meal organised for the two of us."

"Cool, but hey, if that's the case then why are you here?"

"My boss called in to ask if I could do the lunchtime shift, apparently the regular guy phoned in sick, so I agreed, providing I could finish at five, to give me time to get home and get ready to go out. I get here and it's stupidly busy, and then the regular evening barman phones in sick as well, my boss goes into a panic, begs me work the evening."

"I hope you refused."

"Yes I did, but then he threatened to sack me if I didn't."

"What? Oh that is low. He can't do that, surely?"

"He can if you work cash in hand. It's a trade off, you give up your employees rights if you work without paying income tax. And right now, I need the money, I can't be out of work. So I had to agree."

"How did the girlfriend take it?"

"Not well. She actually dumped me there and then over the phone."

"Ouch, that's harsh."

"And then this Mick bloke of yours calls in and gives me your message. And then, of course, this lady pours her drink over me."

"Once again, I really am so sorry about that."

"Yes, so, that's been my evening."

"You know what, that is worse than my evening."

Peter looked over at the clock.

"Right, that is officially the end of my shift, I'm going to sneak out of here before my boss tries to make me work until closing time."

"Good move, up to anything interesting tonight?"

"Don't know. Head for home, ready meal, couple of beers then cry myself to sleep as I lament the sad end of my relationship, maybe?"

"Snap, I was going to go home, ready meal, bottle of wine, then lament the non-existent status of my love life. I bloody hate Valentine's night."

"Worst Valentine's night ever."

"Amen to that." For a few moments they sat in silence.

"You know, we could, possibly, go and get some food – together?" said Peter, slightly uncertainly.

"Not like a date?"

"Oh no, definitely not a date."

"Definitely not, and nothing romantic either, no restaurants."

"Hell no, they'd all be booked out, anyway, it is Valentine's night after all."

"How does a kebab sound?"

"That sounds unromantically wonderful, let's go."

And with that Zara and Peter headed for the exit together. Zara looked back and saw the red carnation. She'd left it lying atop of the bar, now looking very sorry for itself and a bit soggy from having been left in a small puddle of beer. *From now on, whenever I see a red carnation I shall always think of you, Mick – you useless prat*, she thought. But then she glanced back at Peter and smiled. *Ah well, maybe Valentine's night won't turn out to be so bad after all.*

# CAT NAP

Damian Garside


no man is an island he
thought and
dreamt
sleeping between his wife (soft
promontory)
and surreptitious sneak of a pet cat
there, quietly, decisively
to watch his back

# KILLING TIME

Andy Whitson

Midnight, Philip's not back.

I get up to pee and hear him land from the balcony. He appears at the door (his command to be let in), but no customary meow. Bleary-eyed I obey.

Suddenly he bolts; four tiny legs replicating a centipede's. There's a thud, scuttling of tinier feet and a squeak. It's a live present - a mouse.

I shut the pair in the hallway.

*God damn it!* I think, standing bare footed in my pants. I peer through the kitchen hatch killing time to devise a plan.

Several chases and squeaks later an idea comes. I don an insulated glove and grab a kitchen cloth.

With the mouse in hand I run to the balcony and launch it into the night sky and to the bushes below.

Philip sniffs what's left of the mouse; I drag myself off to bed to escape my tiredness.

# RIVERCHILD

Patti Ludwig

She dragged herself out of the river with the aid of the tree against which she had come to ground. Still draped over gnarled roots, she coughed out the water she'd inhaled. Bouts of shivering took her when not vomiting more water. Her people did not swim, jumping had been desperation.

The newcomers were predators, whatever soft words they had offered when they arrived in the hamlet. The fact that they'd chased her into the river sealed it.

She had been the one who recognized which of the village dogs had taken to killing chickens, and proved it. She had known the animal would escalate its victims. The chief Shepard had agreed, and overruled the dog's owner to destroy it.

So why had no-one listened when she told them that these so called traders were killers too? Not even after the first child had disappeared. Nor after the second one. But she had known Harmon. He had been bold, yes, but he had also listened to serious warnings of real dangers, much as she had done at his age. Dismissing his disappearance as his own adventurous nature was blindness, fostered by the dazzling opportunities the newcomers were suggesting to her people.

"Halloo!" The voice was distant, but she froze anyway for a moment. Was she still near enough home for it to be the enemy? She looked around, but could gain no clue from what she saw.

A few legitimate traders did travel the river, but no villagers ever went down-current with them, so the perspective was unfamiliar, territory she ought to know or not. She shivered, belated reaction to the drawn knives and burning expressions that she had fled by the only route they had left her, as well as chill from the silt filled water weighing her clothing.

A second voice called, and her shivers became shudders, between soaked drowning and fear. Looking around with cover in mind, she pulled herself higher on the great root structure. She gave the grasped root an appreciative pat. Sometimes big trees like this had a hollow amid their roots. As small as she was, she fit into spaces most would reject as only room enough for a toddler escaped from her leading strings.

She gave the rough bark another caress. "With thanks for the grace of catching me, ancient mother, I beg your protection yet again. Shield me from those who search, and their intent be ill," she murmured, voice rough from ejecting the water.

Hoping she wasn't leaving an obvious, sopping trail, she scrambled toward the bole of the tree, sliding and scraping her water-wrinkled hands. A foothold gave way abruptly, and she pitched forward, finding her arms plunged into just such a hollow as she had hoped to find. Worming into it, she found it went up and up, above the water at a slight slope. It opened into what might almost have been a planned den, a slight ridge keeping the bottom of the chamber from dropping immediately off to the tunnel. In the dark, her hands informed her that it was almost a whole arm length taller than her head when she sat on the lip of the slope. Her fingertips, spread to either side, just brushed the dry wood. There even seemed to be some soft duff of – well, she wasn't going to explore closely what the components of the bedding comprised. Enough that she would not be trying to rest on hard bare heart wood.

The muffled river sounds and the dry warmth twined with her fear depleted exhaustion, and she curled into the nest, barely remembering to offer the appropriate thanks-prayer. "For your welcome and protection, my thanks. May I give back five-fold."

She woke slowly, thinking her mother had been speaking to her. It must have been a dream, she thought, stretching luxuriously. Her mother had not used such tender tones to her since she'd been in leading strings herself, more than a decade ago. Last time her mother had spoken to her, her voice had been sharp, tone dismissive of her warnings about the new traders.

Those traders! She dug her claws through the shreds of bark to the solid wood under it, digging with one foreleg and then the other in fury.

Claws? She blinked, realizing that light was reflected up dimly into her refuge, and she was seeing far more than she should by it. Seeing dark furred limbs, the paws buried in the bedding she had lately lain on. At the lower edges of her vision were whiskers stretching from a muzzle she had not had when she entered the tree!

The chamber seemed larger, too, and a chill crept through her limbs as she remembered some of the old tales. Slowly, she turned her head, finding that she could turn it a very great distance. Fearing, but guessing what she would find, she looked down her shoulder. It was hard to make out what she saw, until movement caught her eye, and she followed the lashing tail to the root, then back up the body until she was staring at her own shoulder, sheathed in the dark camouflage of a dapplecat's pelt. She caught her breath, and it was a soft snarl.

Oh. Oh, World-Mother! She had been taken at her word. She sank to her belly, limbs refusing to hold her.

*Peace. Peace, Riverchild.* The voice was that she'd woken to, warmly maternal and indulgent.

Her shocked utterance in reply shook her further, emerging as something that resembled a distressed kitten's mewl.

*Peace*, the mind voice repeated, pressing the quality on her lightly, like her father's hand stroking her hair after her first beau had broken up with her and she had cried into his chest.

*This is a bargain you will find to your liking, in time. Did you not wish to protect your charges as fiercely as the cat her kits? The chance is yours now, though the number of your charges is larger now, Daughter.*

"But I'm no fighter! I'm too small!" she cried out, the words sounding like nothing human.

The voice chuckled, making the tree vibrate softly. *Is the bear sow a greater danger than the dam dapplecat? Would your life to now have suited you to the fighting style of the bear? As you have done before, you may do now, with more speed and greater flexibility, using surprise to get the better of those who would hunt your folk. Is it not what you wished, Riverchild?*

And the Guardian lifted her head, baring sharp teeth in a YES.

# SHIFTING SANDS

Chrissey Harrison

Crisp, brittle dune grass scratched against my jeans as I hiked up the slope. Molly followed behind on her leash, head down, her soft, floppy ears drooping even more than normal. I reached the top of the dune and scanned the horizon; nothing but more dunes as far as I could see in one direction.

Pale, sickly sunlight filtered through the thickening clouds that had drifted in from the coast in the last half hour. It didn't look like rain, but a growing wind pressed my thin check shirt to my body and I hugged my goose pimpled arms across my stomach.

I glanced down at Molly, lying on her belly with her muzzle resting on her paws.

"Oh fine, you can go off the leash, just for a little while."

Her ears perked up and she lifted her head, tail wagging. I unclipped the leash and she shot off down the dune like a greyhound rather than a border collie.

I followed her slowly, my legs already tired from the walk out here on the shifting sands.

"Molly?"

I kept going, following the little dimples of her paw prints. After a few minutes I crested another dune and met a line of black stones stretching left and right. Locals called them the spectre wall and they encompassed a whole swathe of dunes. There were many legends and folk tales about the land inside; some just said the area was haunted, others that the dunes moved and changed, trapping travellers within.

In truth there was just some magnetic anomaly which confused migrating birds. If you took a compass over the spectre wall it would spin in circles. Even so, I rarely went over the line of dark, foot high stones. Something about the place gave me the creeps

I spotted Molly at the base of the next dune. "We're not going that way. Come on."

I needed to get home soon. My mother, bless her, had set me up on a blind date. Another one. For some reason she'd decided twenty eight was too old to be single. I didn't mind. Much. The men she picked for me were all nice guys; grown up, sensible, doing okay for themselves and totally inoffensive. Otherwise known as boring. Their mild, vague charm usually provided adequate company for a single date, but no more than that.

Molly looked at me for a moment and then darted further into the dunes like we were playing a game.

"You... you know some border collies get to be sheep dogs because they are supposed to be very obedient and easy to train. Think about that you useless mutt!"

I stepped through a gap between the stones of the spectre wall, trotted down the dune and took off after her. Every time I reached the top of the dune she was waiting on the next, mocking me. I reached the top of a particularly steep hill and stood with my hands braced on my knees, panting.

"Molly, please just come here." While it wasn't like I was desperate to meet whoever my mother had found for me, I couldn't stand letting people down.

I heard Molly bark and looked up. The sun was dipping low now and I squinted against the glare, even though the clouds softened and diffused the yellow light. A dark figure stood atop the next dune, motionless. Molly growled, low and menacing.

I strained forward, shading my eyes, trying to see the figure more clearly, but the sand under my feet shifted. I shrieked as I lost my balance and fell, rolling down the side of the dune. When I came to a rest at the bottom I lay there for a moment, gulping down air.

I looked up towards the figure and saw a small, stunted tree silhouetted against the grey sky. I rested my forearm across my eyes and took a moment to gather myself.

Warm, moist breath on my chin made me chuckle. I put my arms around Molly as she licked my face, checking I was okay.

"Come on, let's go home."

I clipped the leash back on and led her up the dune, heading back the way we'd come. We crossed one rise and then Molly started tugging me sideways, back into the dune field.

"No, this way, come on Molly." I pulled her after me, ignoring her whining.

We kept walking and the dunes, with their clumps of crackly grass and a few tenacious weeds, began to blend into one indistinguishable mass. After twenty minutes I began to suspect I'd lost my bearings; the dunes weren't that big and it shouldn't have taken that long to cross them.

A dark shape appeared on the next dune. As we got closer I saw it was the same stunted little tree. How could I have gone in a circle?

Molly fretted on the leash.

"It's okay girl. Look, we just need to head this way and stay in a straight line this time."

I orientated myself with the tree to my back, facing the way I was sure we'd come in the first time and gasped. Another dark shape stood on the next rise. I watched it for a moment, not even daring to exhale. Molly growled.

Not a tree this time. The dark figure had the shape of a man clothed in a ragged, black cloak and cowl. I couldn't tell how tall he was; the uniform, featureless dunes distorted size and distance.

I looked away for a moment and when I looked back the figure stood a few paces closer. My chest tightened and I clutched Molly's leash until my hand hurt. Another blink, another pace closer.

I ran, stumbling down the unstable ground and clawing my way up the next slope. Molly bounded along behind me, yapping and snarling at the cloaked figure. My throat dried up from the parched air making me cough and my legs began to tremble from the exertion.

Drawing in air in ragged heaves I pushed myself on. Every time I looked over my shoulder I saw the spectre closing on me. Head down I scrambled up another dune and then looked up into the twisted, scrawny branches of the tiny tree.

A strangled sob rose in my throat. "Shit!"

Molly tugged me off to the side and I stumbled after her, knowing only that I had to keep moving.

On the next dune I caught my toe on a clump of grass, tripped and tumbled down the slope, losing my grip on Molly's leash. I closed my eyes against the flying sand and finally came to a halt at the bottom. Tears streamed down my face and I rolled onto my front, coughing.

Hands grabbed me around the waist and I screamed.

"Whoa, whoa, it's okay!"

I looked round found a man in baggy board shorts and a t-shirt, and not a spectre in black.

"There was, I mean, I thought there was something, someone, following me," I sobbed.

The man looked over my shoulder up the dune. "Well I can't see anything. Are you okay?"

"I'm fine, but... my dog." I looked round. "Molly?"

"We'll find her. What's your name?"

"Laura."

"I'm Kevin. Are you local? Maybe you can help me. I got a bit turned around and I can't find my way off this bloody dune field."

"Me neither. I mean I am local, but I'm just as lost as you at the moment."

He stood and offered me a hand to pull me to my feet. I brushed the sand off. I felt kind of silly now. The spectre haunting me must have just been Kevin and the low light made his figure look like a dark silhouette.

I followed him up a dune, grateful just to have some company in this uncanny place.

"Molly? Here girl." I had no idea which way she'd gone, but she would be able to follow me more easily than I could follow her so she'd find me when she was ready to come back.

"So were you just walking your dog?" Kevin asked.

"Oh, yeah, I walk on the dunes every day but I don't usually cross over the... I mean I don't come this far down the coast. You?"

"My mates and I were surfing, I was going to pick up some food and thought I'd take a shortcut, the dunes didn't seem that wide on the drive in. Not a very short shortcut in the end."

He smiled and some of my tension melted away. We trudged up and down dunes, trying to keep the sun in the same position. After a few minutes I saw a familiar scrawny shadow.

"No way!" I screamed at the tree. "It's not possible."

Kevin ran his hand over the spiky little branches with their small leaves as if to make sure it was real. He scratched his head. "I don't get it."

He took his phone out and held it up.

"You won't get a signal. There's this funny magnetic thing, phones don't work here." I turned away and looked back at the dunes. "Maybe we could try..." The words dried up in my throat as a dark shape appeared a few peaks away, drifting lazily forwards. "Kevin, look."

He looked along my pointing arm and frowned. "What is that?" He cupped his hands to his mouth "Hello? Can you help us?"

I moved closer almost using him as a shield and put my hand on his arm. "Don't, we should just go."

The shadow drifted closer until we could make out the flowing black rags that encased its body.

"Yeah, maybe you're right."

We picked a new direction, noted the position of the sun and broke into a steady jog. I called for Molly as we went but there was no sign of her.

The spectre followed, getting closer and closer. More dark shapes appeared on the dunes around us. My heartbeat thudded in my ears. Kevin took my hand to drag me, panting and wheezing up the steep slopes. My jelly legs barely had the strength to hold me upright, let alone keep running, but they did. I began to lose track of anything but putting one foot in front of the other.

"No. No, no, NO!" Kevin ran up to the lonely tree and kicked it viciously. "It's not bloody possible."

I collapsed to the ground, gasping, and watched five cloaked black figures closing in on us. Kevin balled his fists and stood with his legs apart. "Whatever you guys want, just forget it! This whole dark robe thing is seriously lame."

The leading spectre reached the bottom of the dune and looked up at us. It had no face under the cowl, just a black hole.

"Jesus Christ!" Kevin pulled me to my feet and pushed me behind him.

The spectre advanced and the air cooled to the point I could see little clouds form in front of my lips. I slid my hand into Kevin's and squeezed it. He squeezed back.

The air thickened into a frigid soup that was hard to draw in. I clutched at my chest, eyes watering. The spectre reached out a hand of pale bone towards me and curled its fingers. The remaining air rushed from my lungs and I clawed at my throat. Kevin pushed me backwards, scratching at his own throat and chest.

"Leave... her..." He swiped at the spectre's outstretched hand but his own passed straight through it.

As darkness crept in from the sides I heard a bark behind me. Molly danced on the next dune in her classic "follow me, play with me" way. I remembered her tugging on the lead trying to take me a different direction; maybe she could see through the illusion of this place. I pulled Kevin away from the spectre and pointed. He nodded and we both fought our way through the clinging, soup-like air until it began to release us from its grasp. I sucked in sweet cold air like a woman dying of thirst finding a clear stream of water.

The silent spectres pursued us as we followed Molly over and around the dunes. She stopped for us to catch up every few minutes. I had no strength to call out to her. Every morsel of air went to powering my failing limbs up the next slope.

The other spectres drew in from the sides. I could almost hear the whisper of the black cloth of their cloaks. My legs felt heavier the closer they came, like wading through syrup.

When I spotted the regular humps of the spectre wall on the horizon I nearly wept. "That's it, that's the edge."

I took my eyes off the ground at my feet, so eager to reach the wall, and slipped. I slid down the dune on my belly, sand shifting under me like a conveyor belt taking me straight into the arms of the spectre.

"Laura. No!" Kevin skidded down the slope after me as I grasped at clumps of grass and tried to dig my feet in. I finally stopped and felt hard, brittle fingers close around my ankle. When I tried to scream the soupy air sucked the sound away like a vacuum.

My ankle burned in the icy grip, numbness travelling up my calf to my knee. Kevin grabbed both my hands and hauled me up the slope. I kicked out with my other foot and the spectre lost its grip. I couldn't feel my leg at all.

Kevin half dragged, half carried me until we passed over the line between reality and the uncanny world of the dunes. The spectres fell back and their motions became jerky and agitated; robbed of their prey.

I collapsed into a puddle of aching flesh and trembling nerves. Kevin paced, looking back the way we'd come as Molly bounded up to me. Warmth slowly seeped back into my leg and the feeling returned.

"Are we safe now?"

"I think so." I hugged Molly, rubbed her floppy ears and buried my face in the scruff of her neck. "Good girl. You are such a good girl."

She broke away to sniff around Kevin's shoes and then sat on her haunches looking up at him with her head cocked to one side. He patted her gently and her tongue lolled in a puppy grin.

I staggered to my feet. "I'm sorry, she's a shameless flirt."

"Oh yeah?" He gave her another rub around the ears and then stepped closer to me. "What about you?"

"I er..." I looked up and he stroked my hair from my face, brushing my cheek with his thumb. Funny how I suddenly couldn't breathe again.

# TO STRUGGLE

Chrissey Harrison

Why resist,
When I am clay in your hands to mould?
You forge my shape

Why hope,
When tears elicit no pity or mercy?
You are cold to me.

Why try,
When all the ways out are closed off?
You hold all the keys.

Why play,
When it always plays out the same way?
You win and I lose.

Why?
Because.

# RECKLESS LOVE

Amy Cummins

I loved you without caution,
Though I knew you belonged to another.

I loved you without warning,
But to me it was no bother.

Then my world was shattered,
My heart broken in two.

There were many mere girls,
Like me.

I felt like such a fool.
My soul in pieces.
My mind unglued.

Why did I delude myself,
Let myself believe,
I was meant for you?

# ROMANCE IN WHITE GOWNS

Sophie Jackson

Stephanie felt the cup slip out of her unresisting fingers and splash water across the tray. A small sob almost escaped her lips at the sight of it, at the knowledge of how weak her left hand had become since the accident.

She grabbed tissues from the bedside cupboard and began mopping the spill, hoping none of the other patients had noticed the mistake. The doctors had told her to learn to do things with her right hand instead of the left, which had been crushed when she came off her motorcycle, but she had always been left-handed and she didn't want to change. It was too hard, it didn't feel right.

She managed to get the tissues into the bin beside her bed just as the first arrivals for visiting time appeared in the ward. Smiling people, spouses, parents, siblings, children, all come to see someone. Stephanie glanced forlornly at the passage of visitors. She had no family to visit her or, at least, she didn't remember any family. Everything before the accident was a blank, and no parents or siblings had shown up to claim her.

Those first few visiting times had been awful. Watching the clock as the other patients talked with loved ones, cringing at happy laughter, close to tears when someone offered comfort or compassion. She had no idea if she had been lonely before the accident, but she certainly was now.

And then a smiling young man turned up at her bed one day with a bunch of flowers from the hospital shop. She had no idea who he was. He called himself Ed and sat down beside her. He was so good-looking and charming. Stephanie didn't feel such a mess when he looked at her, even though she did self-consciously pat at her bed-flattened hair. He stayed the whole hour and then left promising to come again when he could.

He had been so nice. She watched him leave, missing his welcome presence already and so grateful to the handsome stranger who had bothered to stop and talk with her. She supposed he was one of the volunteers who popped into the hospital to spend time with patients who were alone during visiting time. Someone, a nurse probably, had noticed her loneliness. She felt quite emotional at the kindness of such people and had no way of knowing how she could thank him. Just saying the words didn't seem enough.

He came back four days later, just when she had given up hope of seeing him again. When he walked onto the ward her heart began to beat faster and faster, she wanted to jump out of the bed and run over like an excited child. Stephanie couldn't believe how rapidly she was falling for this kindly man.

He brought some books this time.

"I hope you like them." He said, "Wasn't sure what you read."

She told him anything that helped pass the long hours on the ward was appreciated. Then they stumbled into silence. Perhaps it was her sudden infatuation for him that made conversation abruptly awkward. They started to debate the weather, which she knew was a bad sign and, without thinking, she reached for a cup of water with her left hand. Of course her fingers failed her and she spilt water all over him.

"I'm so sorry!" Stephanie was so mortified she started to cry.

She was so embarrassed by her battered body which no longer obeyed her control. But the handsome stranger only laughed.

"Don't be silly." He grinned. "A little water never hurt anyone."

"The doctors say I will never get the full use back in this hand and I have to learn to use the other one more." Stephanie desperately explained, clenching her bad left hand into an awkward fist.

To her surprised Ed took her hand and gently opened it.

"Doctors don't know everything." He said, rubbing her fingers gently, "Gosh, your hand is cold."

"Cold hands, warm heart." Stephanie said automatically and then she blushed bright red.

After that they slipped back into conversation like they were old friends and Stephanie felt so much better when Ed left that she almost begged him to come back the next day, but resisted. Surely he had other people he visited and who needed him so badly too.

And now it was the day before she was due to be sent home. If Ed didn't turn up today she would never see him again. Her heart sank to the pit of her stomach, the thought of never seeing his smile again hurt her more than she could have imagined.

It seemed all the visitors who had been waiting had come onto the ward and there was no Ed. She looked at the doors hopefully for a few seconds after the last person had come in, then sighed and hung her head so she didn't have to look at the other patients. She toyed with a fragment of tissue left in her lap.

"You look rather miserable for someone who is going home tomorrow."

Stephanie looked up and there he was, walking towards her with a fluffy teddy bear in his arms.

"I know you don't really need another gift." He said apologetically as he handed it over.

"Ed!" Stephanie's spirits soared for a second and then came crashing down, "Oh, but I go home tomorrow."

"Isn't that good?" Ed asked.

"Of course! But..." Stephanie sighed and then blurted out, "Oh, but I won't see you again!"

Ed sat down beside her, a strange look on his face.

"Do you know who I am Stephanie?"

"One of the hospital volunteers who visit people with no family." Stephanie said, gnawing on her lip at the look in Ed's eyes.

"The doctors said the memory loss could be severe, but I didn't realise..." Ed suddenly looked emotional. "I thought the way you talked you remembered me."

"Remember you?" Stephanie stared at him, but she couldn't fill that black gulf in her memory, "I don't remember anything except spinning off my bike. I only know my name because the nurse told me."

"Stephanie..." There was a catch in Ed's throat, "I'm your husband."

He showed her his wedding ring, instantly Stephanie glanced down at her own damaged hand.

"They had to cut your ring off." Ed swallowed hard as if holding back tears. "Do you remember nothing?"

Stephanie stared at him again, longer this time, harder. She remembered the fast beating of her heart when she first saw him, the elation of his presence, the disappointment when he left.

"I don't remember things," she said, trying so hard to explain. "Not pictures. But, I remember emotions and I remember from the first time I met you I fell in love with you. When you walk in this ward it's like... it's like, everything gets brighter."

A smile slowly crept back onto Ed's face.

"And now I learn I get to come home with you!" Stephanie laughed. "That's like Christmas, no better than Christmas, because it's all the time, forever."

She grabbed his hand.

"If you don't mind having a lop-sided wreck living with you of course," she added.

Ed's eyes were sparkling with unshed tears. Impulsively he leaned forward and kissed her on the lips. It was as though a light flicked on in Stephanie's brain and suddenly everything felt right. She remembered Ed's smell, the feel of his lips, the touch of his hair brushing her skin. She remembered how they would walk hand-in-hand, the way he snorted when he laughed hard and the cute wrinkles that would draw in his forehead when he sulked. He pulled back and just stared at her smiling.

"But there is one thing I don't understand." Stephanie felt uncertainty grip her. "Why haven't you visited me more often?"

"Oh that's simple." Ed squeezed her hand, "I had to get someone to look after Dotty and that wasn't easy to do."

"Dotty?"

"Please remember her, Steph." Ed was pleading, "Dotty. Dorothy. Our baby girl."

Stephanie's mouth formed an 'O' of surprise and then understanding. Dotty! For a second a memory of the smell of baby skin and talcum powder filled her mind and then there it was – the image of her little girl all smiles and dimples.

"Dotty! But it's her birthday tomorrow!" She said.

Ed couldn't help but grin.

"Don't worry, you'll be home for it. The best birthday gift for a little girl is her mum home."

Stephanie cried out with delight and flung her arms around him.

"Please tell me this isn't a dream."

"It isn't."

She clung tightly to him.

"I love you Ed."

He kissed her ear.

"I love you Steph." Then for a moment he went serious, "And don't you ever get on a motorbike again."

Stephanie chuckled.

"Motorbikes? I'm sorry Ed, I can't seem to remember what they are."

Ed rolled his eyes in fake exasperation and hugged her hard.

# STARLIGHT

Gareth Wilson

We often hear of constant involvement
Of how time and space collide
Where we're mere whispers of dust in the wind
Compared to the starlight that sails by
So if it evolves as we revolve
Spending our microsecond watching
What does light become?

# THE CARDINAL RUINS

Heidi Hovis

"So they camp by these ruins of an old settlement. They go to check them out and bang a lot of stuff, move some logs, looking for anything good, I swear it was like they were expecting to find gold." Lucas was telling the story.

I was only half listening and feeling a little bored as I looked around the campsite and knew that the ruins weren't that far away. My grandpa had said that I should be able to smell them.

"They never found nothing but that night as they're sleeping, all peaceful like, they hear it. Like someone scratching at a wooden door. They were all too scared to go see what it was. The next morning they finally got up the nerve to have another look."

I was a bit more interested now because I had never heard this side of the story before and had always wondered how they had found him.

"They went cabin by cabin, then they found one that was all burnt up except the floor. They found an old cellar door with this big rusty lock on it. Most of them didn't want to open it cuz they figured it was just an old root cellar but this guy Robert was convinced that there was treasure there. So he goes to get an axe and hammers away at the lock until it breaks. The stench sends most of them running away, cuz it reeks like hell. Robert is like crazy into it though. He comes running out puking everywhere, says it was just old rotting bones. He figured that the people were locked in there to die."

I shivered as I remembered my grandpa's story; just thinking of being trapped with a bunch of dead rotting bodies for so long would make anyone crazy, especially a werewolf.

"They all went to bed and were never seen again. When the cops showed up there weren't no one there, like they all vanished, but the cops snoop around and find the ruins. The cabin with the cellar door is all covered up again but they dig it out."

"They find them, everyone dead and half eaten and stuffed down that cellar with all the other bones. They bring in the big city detectives but they never find anything. Then Robert comes out of the woods on the other side of highway 63, he's totally crazed. Babbles about wolves and big red eyes, killing them all. The cops take one look at him and figure he'd done it, killed them and stuffed them in the cellar. Newspapers talked about some smell coming from the cellar that made him go crazy, they came up with lots of reasons why it was him. But the thing is, there's no way he could've moved those logs to cover up that cellar, it took a few tow trucks to pull them off. So that guy Robert's sitting in the loony bin while the real killer, what wuz trapped in that cellar is free now, and after being down there for like a hundred years, it's crazy hungry."

Lucas looked around at the boys now, his eyes wide with excitement as he ended the story.

"I bet yas, he's still out here, that thing that howled like a wolf, and he's hungry and just waiting for someone else to come by, he's got a taste for people now."

"What do you think Ian?" Josh turned to me and asked, I had to shake myself to stop thinking of that wolf, he'd gone crazy all right, still would be if they hadn't had to kill him to keep the peace.

"Yeah your people are from around here aren't they?" Bryan asked trying not to sound condescending when he said 'your people' and failing slightly.

Maybe that pissed me off, or thinking of my grandpa's friend being trapped like that, whatever it was, I got it in my head to play with them that night.

"My people tell stories of some pretty mean wolves in these parts so yeah maybe he's still around, just stay real close to the tents and if you hear anything, run for the van." I said; letting my eyes get wide like Lucas had, make it look like I was maybe a bit scared.

"Ok, guys, enough ghost stories, you'll all be peeing your sleeping bags." Patrick, their leader, said.

# THE CARDINAL RUINS

I was sharing a tent with Lucas and waited until he started to snore before I snuck out. All the other tents were quiet. There were six tents for us kids, two to a tent and one for Patrick.

I didn't make a sound as I walked into the woods. I found a little clearing and stripped off my clothes to change. I grunted as my bones popped in and out and my body contorted in on itself, before I could breathe again through my snout.

I stretched and I sat back to howl as loud as I could. I heard the guys screaming already and started back. I figured if I let them see me and growl at them a bit, it would be enough to make them all pee their pants and run for the van.

It all worked perfectly, I was trying hard not to laugh as I watched them scurry and scream their way to the van that was locked but I wasn't counting on Patrick having a shot gun.

I saw him come out with it and turned to run but he caught me across the back and I had to stop him. I meant to just grab the gun from him but when I jumped at him he moved and my mouth closed on his arm; I tasted blood.

I jumped off him and was going to run into the woods but the guys had found some guts and were all standing around me with sticks in their hands. They went to swing at me and I lost it; between the pain on my back and the blood in my mouth, it was too much for me to stand. Everything went red and all I remember is their screams and the taste of their blood.

When I woke up I was covered in blood. I did the only thing I could think of, I dragged their bodies to the cellar and locked them in. Grandpa was going to kill me when he found out what had happened but I was pretty sure he'd rather me do this then leave all the evidence and have the police looking for a killer wolf.

I cleaned up the campsite and made it look like they had vanished, then I went to the van and called the police. They came and found me, with gunshot wounds on my back and one in my leg, and believed my story of trying to play a joke on the boys and Patrick shooting me. I said I didn't remember what happened next and woke up alone.

They found the boys in the cellar; they even found Patrick, crazed by highway 63 a few days later. They've since shut down the area and burned it down, cabins, cellar and everything. No one's allowed to camp there anymore and no one wants to. They say the place is haunted and they're not wrong.

# BLOOD OF THE MOON

Amy Cummins

For nights on end,
The sky was red,
As though the moon had been stabbed
And was bleeding.
Then suddenly the stars appeared,
So I wished and prayed,
For love to be given me.
But again the sky turned scarlet,
And my heart sank behind a cloud.
Then the moon shone bright
And a star burned through my window.

# THAT SUMMER AT THE LAKE

Chrissey Harrison

*Based on an original concept by Simo Muinonen.*

A minnow nibbled on Kelsy's tail fin where it dangled in the water. It tickled, but she held perfectly still so she wouldn't scare it away. Summer was always her favourite time of year. She could spend hours lying on the rocks in the sun, just listening to the birds and crickets on the shore.

When she was younger she'd had to be careful around this end of the lake, in case she was seen, but the family that owned the isolated summer house on the bank hadn't visited in years. She enjoyed the extra freedom, but she missed them sometimes. Humans were fascinating; able to come and go as they wished, the whole world to explore.

She closed her eyes, tilted her head back to catch the sun on her face and smiled at the nibbling minnow still pecking at her tail.

A crunch of gravel startled her. She turned her head slowly. No sudden movements; a bear could happily make a good meal out of a young mermaid. A rhythmic tap accompanied approaching steps. On the shore, barely thirty meters away, a human approached the wooden jetty. When he looked the other way she flattened herself on her stomach against the rocks. The shape of the rocks would conceal her upper body and her tail would blend against the grey unless the light caught it. If she tried to slide back into the water he would see her. She peered past the rock and watched for an opportunity.

In his right hand the human held a white stick, long and slender. He tapped a post of the jetty with the tip of the stick and then stepped forward with his left hand out-stretched. With the stick dangling from his wrist by a thin strap he placed both hands on the edge of the jetty and worked his way along towards the landward end.

He looked familiar. Kelsy lifted her head for a better look. He reminded her of the boy who'd visited every summer when she was younger, but he was much bigger than that boy; taller and broader in the chest. He had the same dark coloured hair as the boy, but his was longer and not as tidy. It couldn't be the same person. But then, she supposed humans grew up in the same way as her own kind. Maybe it was him. It had been four, maybe even five years since she'd last seen him.

He felt his way along the jetty and climbed up onto the wooden platform. He stood and gently tapped the edges with his stick. Slowly, he walked out towards the water end, staring at an unfixed point ahead of him. Kelsy's head rose a fraction more. He wasn't looking at the jetty, nor at anything in particular. His steps were slow but steady, and he wasn't slowing down as he approached the end. Was he just going to walk off into the water? His stick flicked past the last post and he took a hasty step back, left hand thrown out to the side.

He hadn't known how close the end was until his stick met air rather than wood. The boy she'd seen when she was young hadn't been blind, but she felt sure it was him.

She silently lifted herself back to a sitting position and watched him. He lowered himself onto the jetty, pulled off his shoes and gingerly shifted forwards until his legs dangled over the end and the water lapped around his ankles.

Kelsy slid off the rock into the water with a gentle splash and surfaced again immediately.

"Hello?" the human called. "Is someone there?"

She drifted a little closer, soft flicks of her tail all that she needed to keep at the surface.

"Is someone swimming?"

Kelsy licked her lips. He knew she was there, but he couldn't see her, couldn't see what she was. He would never be able to tell that she wasn't just a human swimming. "I am," she said.

A soft frown flickered across his face. "Do you want me to go?"

A twitch of her tail brought her to the base of the jetty. "No." His face was still soft and youthful, with a couple of little red marks and a hint of dark hair cut back to the skin. Her own kind reached adulthood around their fifteenth year. She was just there herself; fully grown even if she wasn't treated like it. What was the human, a boy or a man? Or was he like her, just on the cusp between childhood and adulthood?

"Are you still there?" he asked.

"Yes."

"What's your name? I didn't think anyone else ever came here." He kept his face turned to her, but his eyes never fixed on her or anything.

"Kelsy. Who are you?"

"Boyd Vass, my family owns the house back there." He gestured over his shoulder.

"It's nice to meet you, Boydvass."

He chuckled. "No, it's just Boyd. Vass is my surname. Don't you have a surname?"

"Huh?"

"You know, a second name, a family name?"

"My name is Kelsy."

"Just Kelsy?"

"Yes."

"Well then it's nice to meet you too, just Kelsy."

He smiled. Kelsy wasn't sure she was following him.

"Do you live round here?" he asked.

"Umm, yes. I live here."

"Where?"

"Here."

"No, I mean where's your house?"

She shrank back from him a little. "On the west bank. I live with my... grandmother. I... I should go." She ducked under and powered through the water with one swift tail stroke, then surfaced and looked back at him still sat on the end of the jetty.

"Wait," he called. "Will you come back? Kelsy?"

"I don't know. I have to go now. Goodbye."

The water swallowed her up and she struck out for home, safe in the depths of the lake.

\* \* \*

Even down in the depths Kelsy could see clearly; when only a fraction of the daylight made it down to the depths, and even less moonlight, eyes that could see in very low light were essential. Kelsy thought the humans had it right with their artificial lights.

Dome shaped dwellings, built from rounded river rocks covered the lake bed. Kelsy thought they looked like tombs as she approached from the bright world above. No welcoming lights, no heat and a constant battle to keep the silt out. Why they didn't just sleep in the mud she didn't know. It seemed so primordial, like they were little more than animals. Maybe they were.

"Kelsy!"

She fanned her tail and stopped dead. "Mother?"

Her mother's pale face appeared at the door to their shared dwelling. "Inside. Now!"

Her heart pattered against her ribs. How did she know? Inside her mother backed her up against the far wall.

"Kelsy, we have rules for a reason. To keep you safe. Whatever were you thinking?"

How could she know? Maybe this was about something else. "What did I do?"

He mother's eyes flashed daggers. "You were seen! By a human. From what Lillia tells me you did it on purpose. Carelessness I could forgive, but this!"

"I wasn't seen." Which was technically true. "The human can't see, therefore I couldn't have been seen."

"That is hardly the point. You made contact, revealed yourself."

"So what? He thought I was just a human girl."

"And how long were you planning to keep up such a ruse?"

Kelsy frowned. She hadn't planned any of it. She knew how dangerous it could be if he figured it out. She'd left, hadn't she? Did her mother really think she was so reckless that she would have done it again? And if that was what she thought anyway, what would it matter if she did go back? He mother had obviously already made up her mind that she couldn't be trusted.

"I forbid you from seeing that boy again. Do you understand me, Kelsy?"

She nodded. She understood perfectly.

The next morning Kelsy's head broke the surface in the centre of a shallow ripple which spread out across the mirror surface of the lake. A light mist still hung low over the water.

She hadn't expected Boyd to be there. She'd been taught that humans were lazy creatures who slept the day away and then burned their lights into the night hours. But there he was, sat on the end of the jetty once more. She could have believed he hadn't moved were it not that he wore different garments.

The change brought to mind her own lack of clothing. Attuned to the temperature of the lake her body didn't need clothing to keep warm and there was no modesty among her people. As she swam closer to the boy on the jetty she wondered what his reaction would be if he could see her. Would he be shocked, offended? Humans seemed very insistent on covering up.

He didn't react to her approach, although she made plenty of noise. Not until she was within a few meters did she notice the little white pods in his ears.

She moved closer, studying him. His unfocused eyes were slightly unsettling. In her experience, only the very old lost their sight, and then their eyes turned cloudy white. They didn't look like normal eyes. Boyd's looked like normal eyes, but like there was nothing behind them. Like glass eyes, perhaps.

Close enough to reach out and touch him she caught a whisper of sound; a tinny, scratchy whine on the edge of hearing. She tipped her head one way then the other and decided the sound was coming from Boyd.

She put her hand out and brushed her fingers on his calf below his rolled up trousers. He jumped and pulled his legs up onto the jetty. One hand quickly pulled the cabled pods from his ears. "Who's there?" The scratchy sound grew louder.

"Hello Boydvass."

"Kelsy?"

"What are those pod things?"

He paused for a second, rapid breath slowing, and then dangled the pods from his hand. "These?"

"Yes, are they making that noise?"

"You've never seen headphones before?"

"What are they for?"

He disentangled the cords from his clothing and pulled a little white box from his pocket. "I use them to listen to my iPod. Do you want to try?" He held out the headphones but kept the box in a firm grip. "Don't get them wet."

Kelsy smiled, took the headphones and held one to her ear. The faint noise grew until loud, fast-paced music filled her ear. She added the second. It was very noisy, but so exciting. Nothing like the gentle singing of her kind. Ears stoppered up with the headphones blaring away she couldn't hear anything else. No wonder Boyd didn't hear her approach.

"It is very interesting music," she shouted over the din.

Boyd said something else but the words didn't penetrate.

"What?"

He put one hand to his ear and mimed pulling out the headphones. Kelsy removed them.

"I said it's Biffy Clyro."

"What's a biffy clyro?" she asked.

Boyd chuckled. "The band, silly. Boy, you really don't get out much living here." He pressed the iPod and the music stopped.

"Never, actually."

"Do you live here all year?"

"Yes. We get ice on the lake in the winter."

"I've never been here in the winter."

"I know."

His brow creased. "How do you know?"

"You used to visit in the summer, every year. Then you didn't."

He let out a long sigh. "Yeah, after the accident my parents didn't think it would be safe for me here."

"Accident? Is that how you became blind?"

The corner of his mouth quirked up. "You noticed that, huh? I know, it's pretty obvious. And yeah, I was hit by a car; fractured my skull. There was a blood clot and the bit of my brain that dealt with sight got starved of oxygen."

Even on the darkest nights Kelsy's super sensitive eyes could still make out shapes and shadows. She depended so heavily on her eyesight that the thought of being trapped in the dark sent a shiver up her spine. "Does it frighten you?"

"It did at first. I got used it. I still get scared if I'm on my own somewhere I don't know."

Kelsy smiled at the idea of an unknown place. She knew every crevice of the lake, every reed bed, every point where a stream trickled in, every rock and tree along the shore. In her world, unknown was the same as out of reach. It was one thing she envied humans for more than anything, the ability to explore, to get lost.

"Like where?" she asked.

"Anywhere really. My Dad took me to a football game a couple of months back and we got separated."

"Football?"

"Yeah, doesn't make sense does it? A blind guy at a spectator sport. I listened to the radio commentary, but it really wasn't the same. I think Dad wanted to try and make me feel like nothing had changed, but it just highlighted it."

"Hmm." Kelsy chose not to try and explain she'd been asking what football was. Obviously it was something any human should know about.

"How come you're swimming so early?" Boyd asked.

"I like coming up to the surface at dawn, everything seems so full of energy, just waking up to face the day."

"Coming up to the surface? That's a funny way of putting it."

Kelsy's stomach turned an acid flip. "Just something my Grandmother says, I guess." Her voice trembled. "I er... I should be getting back to her actually." She pushed away from the jetty.

"Wait, can I see you again? I mean, you know, can we meet up again?"

"I umm, I don't know."

"Did I say something wrong?"

No, she had. "No, it's nothing. I'm sorry."

She dove and let the water seal her away from him.


None of her extended family would understand, but Kelsy needed someone to talk to. She surfaced near the end of the only other jetty on the lake; a short stubby pier outside an old stone-built cottage. The cottage had been there since the first humans discovered the lake nearly two hundred years ago. By comparison, the Vass' summer house was a toddler.

Kelsy peeked over the end of the jetty towards the house. If Rebecca saw her, then she'd stay, if not, she'd leave. The old woman's figure passed the window but she didn't look out. Kelsy ducked back down. Well that was hardly long enough to tell for sure. She lifted back up and found a smiling face watching her from the window. She waved.

Rebecca wasn't like other humans. Her family had owned the tiny cottage for as long as anyone could remember. They knew of the mermaids and kept their secret. They even traded goods once in a while. It was because of Rebecca that Kelsy knew what shoes were, but not headphones, that humans lit their homes because they couldn't see in the dark, and that they wore clothes to keep warm.

The rear door of the cottage opened. A moment later Rebecca stepped out. She held a paper bag in one hand and an involuntary grin lit up Kelsy's face.

"Hello, child," the old woman said as she stepped onto the jetty. "What brings you here so early in the day?"

"Hello."

Rebecca lowered herself to the planks and sat with her rubber boots just touching the water's surface. She held out the bag of candy and Kelsy took a piece. The tangy sweetness that exploded on her tongue never ceased to bring tears to her eyes. It was just so far from anything and everything she tasted in her own world. From her first visit it had come to symbolise everything that humans were; bright, exciting, enticing.

"Don't tell me you're just here for my candy," Rebecca said with a chuckle.

"I'm sorry. Thank you, for the sweet. I did come for something else."

"And what might that be?"

"What do you know of the family that visit the house on the south shore?"

"The Vasses?"

"Yes. Are they... good?"

"I would say so. I've never had much reason to talk with them. The father is a lawyer, I think, and the mother a teacher."

Kelsy nodded, although she had only a fleeting idea of what a lawyer was.

Rebecca tilted her head to the side. "Why do you ask?"

Kelsy looked down at the surface of the water just below her chin. "I did something foolish, I think."

The old woman stayed silent and the truth burned on Kelsy's tongue. "I spoke to the son, his name is Boyd. He showed me his music, and I touched him and then I said something careless. Now I know I shouldn't go back, in case he guesses, but I want to, and I don't feel like he's dangerous."

"The son? He lost his sight, didn't he?"

Kelsy nodded.

"He doesn't know what you are."

"No, but Mother says any human would kill me, or take me captive if they saw me. She says they all have hateful hearts. Is it really true? I don't think Boyd is like that."

"Do you think I have a hateful heart?" Rebecca asked.

"No, of course not. But Mother says you're different. Your family are like our guardian spirits."

Rebecca chuckled. "What a tall tale. Humans are not all the same, just as merpeople are not all alike. Your mother is right to warn you, some humans are quick to destroy what they do not understand, but not all." She sighed. "Kelsy, I think it is time for you to know a truth, and I think it is unlikely that your family will ever share it with you."

Kelsy's eyes widened. "A secret?"

"Of sorts. Has your mother ever mentioned your aunt Mara?"

"Yes. She was killed by humans when I was very little. I remember her, but Mother doesn't believe me. She says my memories are just what I imagine from what people have told me."

"She wasn't killed."

"But, Mother said—"

"Your mother told you that because she didn't agree with how her sister chose to live her life."

Kelsy's frown deepened. "But if she's alive, where is she?" No merperson left the lake. They couldn't. Rebecca watched her for a moment and she found herself holding her breath with the anticipation.

"She met a man, a human male, and they fell in love. She left to be with him. On the land."

The held breath rushed out and Kelsy sucked in another and another. There was a way to leave. "She—"

"Became human, yes."

"How?" She grasped the edge of the deck.

Rebecca smiled softly. "It is no easy thing, and no easy decision. A change like that is permanent and only possible if one's heart is bound to a land dweller so that it cannot bear to let form keep them apart."

Her mind returned to Boyd sitting on the end of the jetty.

"You mean love."

"Of course. The only force with the power to change the nature of the world."


Kelsy stayed and asked her friend more about the aunt she'd never really know. The reason for her mother's anger suddenly became so clear. She wasn't afraid Kelsy would be hurt, she was afraid she would fall in love with a human and leave as her sister had. Kelsy wasn't sure if that made it better or worse.

The possibility that she could become human took root in her mind and would not be dislodged. Hadn't she always wished she could be free to explore the land? She wondered whether she would choose to leave if it were a simple choice but she wasn't sure. And it wasn't a simple choice. She could only leave if she loved a human, and it had to be real, not some trick to get what she wanted... if it even *was* what she wanted.

She didn't know if she could love Boyd. She wasn't even sure she knew what love should feel like. Her thoughts raged around her head in a confusing tangle. She wanted to see him again. But did she want to see him... or did she just want to see her ticket to a life of adventure?

By the time she reached home she'd made a deal with herself. She'd wait three days, and if she still wanted to see him, she'd go. The riot in her head continued though. She couldn't think of anything else.

Three days later she surfaced beside the empty jetty by the Vass house. She felt a sudden pang of guilt, wondering if he'd waited for her on the days between her visits, but why would he? She hauled herself out of the water onto the end of the jetty and let the sun warm her skin.

An hour or so later she heard the crunch of shingle on the shore. Her stomach fluttered and a warm smile spread over her lips. Then a dart of panic made her lift her head; what if it wasn't Boyd? But it was. He tapped his way towards the jetty with his iPod in one hand.

"Hello Boydvass," Kelsy said with a giggle.

He stopped still. "Hi. Are you swimming again?"

"Not at the moment."

He smiled and her stomach did another of those flutters. She glanced down at the scaled lower part of her body. "Please, don't come too close," she said.

"Okay," he said, and started forwards again.

She felt the sudden urge to cover her chest with her arms and sat up with them folded. It was silly. She never felt such a need with her own people and Boyd couldn't see her. But somehow the thought of him being so close to her body made her feel naked in a way she'd never experienced before.

Boyd tapped his way down the jetty. "Where are you?"

"Just at the end."

His stick swung past a few inches from her scaled hip. "You can sit there, if you like."

She watched the way he folded up his legs as he sat. Legs were funny, the way they bent independently of each other. If she became a human, she'd have legs. That would be very strange indeed.

"Is this okay?" he asked.

"Yes."

He sat stiffly for a moment and then put his iPod in his pocket. "I wasn't sure you'd be back."

"Yeah, I'm sorry. I had some things to do."

"I, er, I hoped you would come back though." He smiled awkwardly. "You know, before I had to go."

The building buzz in Kelsy's stomach suddenly stilled. "You're leaving?"

"Well, yeah. I have to go home, don't I?"

"When?"

"At the end of next week."

His words hung in the air between them. Kelsy wasn't sure what to say. She felt so mixed up inside she didn't think she could untangle her thoughts and figure out if she truly liked him in less than two weeks.

No, that wasn't right. She liked him, she knew that much already.

"Kel, I... er, can I call you that?"

"Okay."

"What do you look like? I hate not being able to picture you in my head."

"Oh, well, um." She glanced down at her tail and cringed. "I have blonde hair."

"Long or short?"

"Long, I guess. And um, my eyes are blue-green, like the water."

He smiled but his eyes looked sad. Kelsy marvelled at how they still held expression, even though they couldn't see. How could she have thought they looked empty before?

"Boyd?"

"Words are just such a poor substitute sometimes." He blinked damp eyelashes.

"What would help?" She thought about how he used his stick to guide him, and the way he navigated with his hands. "Give me your hand." She shifted closer to him, her scales scraping the decking in a way she was sure would sound completely wrong to him. He held his hand out toward her and she took it with hers. He drew in a sharp breath and his lips stayed parted. Kelsy watched him as she raised his hand to her cheek. She held it there a moment then took her hand away and let him feel her. His fingertips softly traced her features. She tried to hold perfectly still. A moment later he brought his other hand up and explored her face with both hands.

His hands felt so warm. Would she feel cold to him? The look of intense concentration on his face made her smile. When he felt the change in her lips and cheeks he smiled too.

"Beautiful," he whispered.

Kelsy realised she was breathing fast, like she'd swum from one end of the lake to the other.

Boyd's hands strayed up into her hair and she closed her eyes. He followed her hair down to her neck and then out across her shoulders.

With a sudden jerk he pulled his hands back and Kelsy's eyes snapped open. "What's wrong?" His face looked as red as sunset clouds.

"Nothing. Thanks, for letting me... thanks."

"That's okay." She was still puzzled about why he stopped and then she put the pieces together. He'd stopped when he felt her bare shoulders when he'd expected to find her wearing clothes. She hugged her arms across her chest again.

Over the summer days that followed Kelsy, met with Boyd whenever she could. Not always for very long; she still had chores and her mother seemed increasingly suspicious about her whereabouts. But she found at least a few minutes every day to speak with him, to fill her eyes with him and to capture that wonderful butter feeling in her stomach. Sometimes they talked, other times he shared his headphones with her so they could listen to his music together.

A few days before he had to leave she visited and found him sitting on the end of the dock listening to a book - he'd shown her how the iPod played stories as well as music - next to a roll of fabric. She stared at the latter, puzzled. He'd also changed out the long trousers for short ones that only came down to his knees, and wore a plain t-shirt.

"Hi," she said, brushing his leg with her hand to let him know where she was.

He quickly pulled his earphones out and put his hand out for her to touch. It was something the two of them had fallen into doing since he'd touched her face; a way to greet each other that was more than just words.

Kelsy squeezed his fingers. "What's that for?" she asked. She pointed and then rolled her eyes at her own hand. "The red cloth thing, I mean."

"It's a towel."

"Oh."

"Sometimes I think you're just winding me up. With all the swimming you do you must know what a towel is."

"Er, yeah, maybe," she said. She'd figure out what the towel was for later.

"Anyway, I thought, well since you love swimming so much, maybe I could swim with you. You might have to help me back after though."

Kelsy's chest tightened. A dizzying mix of excitement and fear rushed through her. She had an idea humans could swim, though only on the surface, and the idea of being in the water with him made her feel warm and fuzzy, but it would only take one brush of her tail, one wash of current from her tail fin, and he would know something was different, wouldn't he?

He took off his t-shirt. Underneath he looked much like the young mermen she knew, but somehow seeing him without his usual coverings felt different, personal; like he was showing her something private. He dipped his toes into the water and lowered himself part way off the jetty then paused. "Promise me you won't leave me," he said.

She realised then what a challenge this was for him. In the water he would have no reference, no stick to guide him. If he went out too far he might not be able to find his way back to the shore. Unless she helped him. He was trusting her to keep him safe. Sharp tears prickled her eyes. "I promise."

He dropped into the water and surfaced again gasping. "Wow, it's freezing."

"You get used to it."

He kicked his legs alternately and circled his hands by his side to keep himself at the surface. Not so efficient as a tail, but he seemed comfortable. Water dripped from his hair down his face. A drop glistened on his lips and he licked them. Kelsy suddenly wanted to kiss him and the dangerous thought made her stomach churn. She couldn't get that close to him. And for all that her people had no qualms about modesty, kissing was something that only couples shared.

She buried the thought. "Swim out with me a bit, I'll guide you back, I promise."

"Okay."

Boyd's swimming was, to her, an awkward thrashing of limbs, every extremity trying to contribute to forward motion and none of them doing a particularly good job. Combined together though he made progress.

She drifted along lazily by his side, watching him. "Have you swum before?"

He slowed a fraction and laughed. "Yes, although it's been a while. Not since before the accident. So don't make fun of me, fish girl."

"I wasn't making fun. I... wait, what did you say?" Her stomach turned to a hard lead lump and she stopped dead in the water. Did he know? How had he figured it out?

"I called you fish girl. You know, because you're always in the water. I figure you must be part fish or something to be able to swim in this every day. I think my toes have gone numb."

"I'm not... I don't..."

Boyd stopped and bobbed in place a few feet from her. "Hey, I was just kidding. I didn't mean to upset you."

Just a joke. Kelsy let herself breathe.

"How far out are we? Feels like miles."

She watched him, the adrenalin of fear draining away. "Not that far, maybe thirty meters."

He grinned at her. "Race you to sixty." He struck out, all limbs flailing and Kelsy giggled to herself.


The next morning she prepared to slip out and greet the dawn as she always did when a hand grabbed her arm from behind.

"No. Not again," her mother said.

Her heart seized. "Not what?" she asked hesitantly.

"You know what. The boy. I said you weren't to see him. You disobeyed me. Hanna saw you with him again yesterday. In the lake!"

Just yesterday? "He doesn't know what I am."

"That's irrelevant. You're asking for trouble, don't you understand that? He will realise soon enough and then you will be in trouble. Humans are dangerous. Remember your aunt, Kelsy. I don't want that to happen to you, you must understand that."

Rage boiled up inside her and she turned slowly to face her mother. "Tell me, Mother, what did happen to my aunt?"

"You know what happened to her."

"Yes, I do. More than you think."

A flicker of uncertainty crossed behind her mother's eyes.

"Were you upset she left you, or were you just jealous that she was happy?"

"Kelsy!"

"Rebecca told me everything. Humans aren't all slovenly gluttonous murderers. I don't even know how I believed you before. And for the record, I've seen Boyd every day this summer, and he still thinks I'm just a human girl. I've been careful, but not because of you." She pulled her arm free of her mother's grasp.

"Don't you dare leave this house."

"I'm sorry, Mom. It's my heart; I have to do what it tells me, even if you tell me not to."

"Your heart? Kelsy, you don't love this boy."

"How do you know? I don't even know. I just know what feels right." She backed up through the doorway with its woven screen of reeds. "Please don't hate me." Then she turned and powered up towards the light.

She burst through the surface of the water and crashed back down with a splash. When she surfaced again she held her hands out level with the water's surface. They shook and she clenched them into fists.

The sun was just peeking over the tops of the surrounding hills. Boyd would probably still be asleep, but that didn't matter, because he wasn't who she needed right now. First she needed Rebecca.

She struck out across the lake and by the time she reached the jetty by the stone cottage she was gasping for breath. She could breathe under water, but her lungs were far more efficient than her small gills. She hauled herself out onto the wooden decking.

"Rebecca?" she called.

There was no sign of movement in the house. It was barely ten meters away. Nothing if she could swim there, but across the short stretch of grass and stone path it might as well have been a thousand miles.

"Rebecca!" she called again.

A few birds took flight from the forest behind the cottage.

Kelsy looked again at the door. So close, but so far. She thought about Boyd and his sightless eyes. How hard it was for him just to move around without tripping or losing his bearings. Yet he'd swum with her, even though it must have been terrifying to not know which way the shore lay. Reaching the door wasn't impossible; it was just difficult and scary.

She pulled herself along the jetty, using her tail to push forwards too. The further she dragged herself from the water the more she felt the panicked urge to go back, to feel its comforting embrace. It was just instinct she told herself, and she was more than that. She was not an animal.

The door approached and her tough scaled tail scraped on the stone path outside. She twisted to sit with her back to the door frame and then pounded her fist on the wood. Glancing back towards the jetty another wave of panic washed through her but she took a few deep breaths. Soft sounds of movement came from within. Then the door opened a crack.

"Oh my goodness, child, what are you doing?"

Kelsy looked up at her over her shoulder. "I need to know how. How do I become human so I can stay with him?"

A faint, slightly sad smile crossed the old woman's lips and she opened the door wider. "Let me get a coat, and we'll talk about it. Go back to the water, child."

The tension in her shoulders flowed away. The answers were coming, but more importantly she could give in to the instinctive need to get back to the water. Crossing back to the shore seemed to take far less time.

A few moments later Rebecca appeared again, wrapped in more clothing. She walked out and lowered herself stiffly to the jetty.

"Tell me how," Kelsy said.

"First tell me why."

"Because I don't want to go back. I want to go with Boyd. He's leaving soon and I can't go back, I can't."

"You remember what I said before?"

Kelsy nodded.

"Then you must realise, it's not enough to want to leave, you have to want to go. Does that make sense?"

Kelsy looked down at the water. All her guilty feelings about seeing Boyd as a ticket away from the life that stifled her rose back up. But no, it wasn't about that. Her fight with her mother was why it had to be now, but she'd already decided she wanted to go with him. The thought of him leaving and not seeing him again for another year, if ever made her stomach churn and her chest tighten. "I understand, and I do want to go, more than anything. It just has to be today, you have to tell me."

Rebecca shook her head and Kelsy's heart sank.

"It cannot be today."

"Why not?"

"Your love and your will make the transformation possible, but it can only happen under a full moon. Such are the ways of magic."

"But, when—"

"Tomorrow night."

"I can't wait that long."

"You have no choice, child. But I will tell you the rest of what you need to know. You will have some preparations to make."

Kelsy nodded eagerly.

"The transformation hinges on a choice. You must make that choice in your heart, but also with an action. A kiss, child. A kiss will seal your fate. And know this; the transformation may work the other way also. Share the kiss on land and both of you will walk away on two legs. Share it in the water and the boy will become your kind."

Boyd could become a merperson? But that wouldn't be right. With no sight he would struggle to fish and they would be trapped together instead of free. It had to be her that made the change.

"I understand."

"Child, are you sure this is what you want?"

Kelsy considered her words carefully then smiled. "With all my heart."

"Good luck."

Rebecca reached a hand out and Kelsy clasped it in her own.

"Go make your plans then."

With a bright smile Kelsy turned and darted away beneath the water.


Boyd greeted her with a grin. "Hey."

"Hi," she swum up to his dangling feet and tickled his toes. His laughter made her feel warm inside.

"Boyd, when are you leaving?" she asked quickly.

His smile faded and he turned away from her. "Sunday."

Kelsy silently thanked the fates. She still had time.

"I want to show you something," she said. A steady jitter filled her stomach. "Meet me here, tomorrow night, after the moon rises."

"At night? Why?"

She touched his foot again, her hand resting lightly. "Please."

He swallowed hard. "Sure, okay."

"You have to do one more thing for me."

"What?"

"And you have to not ask why. I... I promise I'll explain tomorrow, before we... tomorrow. Bring some clothes, okay? Something I could wear."

"You? But—"

"You can't ask why, not yet, okay?"

"Okay, but Kel, why—"

"Tomorrow. Please, Boyd, trust me."

"You know I do."

"I have to go. I'll see you tomorrow."

"Kel, wait."

"I can't stay, they'll... I have to go right now but I'll be back tomorrow, when the moon rises. Promise you'll be here."

"I promise."

She held onto his words as she dove into the depths. Hope and energy sung through her veins. There was only one thing left to do. Hide. If she could avoid her mother for just over a day she would be free. She needed food though, and that meant stopping by the village for supplies for her vigil.

Kelsy cautiously entered her house. It was very quiet. Her mother must be out somewhere. She slipped through the low archway into the chamber which served as a food preparation and storage area. There she took some fish and vegetable cakes and put them in a mesh bag to take with her. She could have fished for fresh food, but she didn't want to risk moving about the lake once she was settled and hidden.

She took a quick look around the rock shelter she'd called home all her life. She wouldn't be coming back. Fear rose up, fear of the unknown but she fought it back down, set her shoulders and started for the door.

A hand clasped around her wrist and then a loop of scratchy rope. She tugged, panicking, then looked behind her. Her mother held the rope. "I'm not letting you leave here, Kelsy." She spiked the back of her wrist with a needle made from a sea urchin spine and the world lurched towards blackness.

A cool night breeze ruffled Boyd's hair. He bounced on the balls of his feet trying to keep warm. The late summer days were warm enough, but the nights cooled off quickly. Kelsy had told him to meet her when the moon rose and he'd agreed. It wasn't until he got inside that he realised he had no idea what time that would be and no way to see.

He looked it up on his laptop - adapted with voice control - and had to trust the time he found was accurate. Not that he had any idea why the moon was important.

The bundle of clothes tucked under his arm - sweatpants and a t-shirt and hoody - felt doubly confusing. Why did Kelsy want him to bring her clothes? She wasn't going to do something stupid, like try to swim all the way from home in the dark, was she?

He rubbed his arms with his hands. Should have worn his coat, but he didn't know where it was and he didn't want to wake his parents by rooting around in the closet.

He strained to listen for any sound of Kel. She had a way of sneaking up on him even when he wasn't using his iPod. She just seemed to pop up out of nowhere. How long should he wait? Should he call?

Minutes ticked by and he sat down on the jetty to wait. The soft lap of the water was soothing and it was already past midnight. He'd been up early, as he usually was, and his eyelids started drooping. He shook his head to wake himself up. "Kel?" he whispered into the night. Where was she? He lay back on the jetty. He'd just rest his eyes for a few minutes.

A hand on his shoulder woke him. He took a moment to wonder why the bed was so hard and it smelled like outdoors. Then he remembered. "Kel?"

"It's Mom, sweetheart."

Shit! He'd slept all night? "Oh, er..."

"What are you doing out here?" A firm edge crept into her voice, one he knew was born of concern, but had no less power to make him feel like he was five because of it.

"I, er, I couldn't sleep. I just wanted some fresh air. I must have nodded off."

"You could have rolled off the jetty in the night, drowned."

"I know. I'm sorry, Mom."

He rubbed his eyes and got to his feet to follow her back to the house. Why hadn't Kelsy come?

He went back out to the jetty after breakfast and stayed there all day. Kelsy didn't make an appearance, and while there had been days when she'd not turned up he was sure she'd come to explain why she hadn't come the night before. As the day drew on he began to hope she'd come by just so he could say goodbye; they were leaving tomorrow.

But she didn't. He went to bed feeling sick in his stomach. Where was she? Why didn't she want to see him? It was hard to meet girls when you couldn't see, especially ones who didn't take pity on you. Kelsy was different. And when she'd said she wanted to meet him at night, even with all the other bizarre requests, well, he'd thought maybe... maybe it was going somewhere.

Now he was leaving in the morning, and he wouldn't even get to say goodbye. Alone in his room he let a few tears soak into his pillow.

"We're all packed, sweetheart," Mom called.

Boyd sat on the end of the jetty. Waiting, praying she'd come to see him off. She knew he was leaving.

His mother's footsteps approached across the shingle. "I know you don't want to go home, but your dad wants to get on the road as soon as we can, so we'll have time to stop for lunch on the way. Won't that be nice?"

"Yeah."

"What's wrong, Boyd?"

He took a deep breath. "Did you know there's another house on the lake, on east side?"

"Yes. I think some old woman lives there."

"There's a girl lives there too, with her grandmother."

"Is that who I saw you with? I thought maybe it was a day tripper."

"You saw—"

"Only briefly. I didn't want to disturb you if you were making new friends."

"Right. Well anyway, she was going to come and say goodbye, but I haven't seen her for two days now."

"Well, would you like to stop by her house before we go? I'm sure your dad wouldn't mind."

He nodded and got up. He was glad he couldn't see the look on her face.

"Boyd, are you and she..."

"I don't know, maybe."

Mom put her arm around his shoulders and squeezed. He leaned against her.

Kelsy's grandmother's cottage was tucked away down a dirt road. Dad drove up, although his car was seriously not designed for off-roading. When he stopped Boyd's stomach started churning. What if he'd done something wrong and Kel really didn't want to see him?

Mom got out and guided him to the door while he tapped with his stick to get a sense of the ground so he could find his way back to the car without her.

"Just call if you need me," she whispered and gave him another squeeze.

She retreated back to the car. Boyd took a deep breath and knocked. It seemed to take forever but eventually someone answered. It wasn't Kelsy.

"Hello, young man," an old voice said.

"Hi, um, is Kelsy home?"

"Home?"

"I mean is she in, is she here? I just... my parents and I are heading home today and I wanted to say goodbye. I'm Boyd, by the way, my family owns the—"

"I know. I'm afraid she's not here."

His heart sank.

"Why don't you come in for a moment?"

"I guess." He stepped forward over the threshold. "Umm, is she okay? She said she'd come to see me, near our place, but she didn't show."

"I'm sure she's fine."

"But, where is she?"

"She comes and goes as she pleases."

"Oh." He scratched the back of his hand nervously and his cane knocked a table leg or something. "Sorry."

"What did she tell you, about me?" the old woman asked.

"She said you were her grandmother, that she lived here. She does live here, right?"

"Well I suppose so, in a way."

Boyd frowned.

"She's not like other girls." Her voice receded as if she were moving around the room.

Boyd stayed put so he wouldn't lose his bearings.

"But then I think you know that, deep down," she continued. "I'm sure when you think about it, all those little things that seemed strange will all start to point in the same direction."

There were strange things about Kelsy. The way she was always swimming, the way she wouldn't let him get too close to her. The way she'd moved through the water when they swam together. Little things.

"I don't know what you mean."

"You will, one day. I'm sorry you didn't get to say goodbye. But, I promise you she will be here if you ever come back."

"Right. Can you tell her I came by?"

"Of course."

He pulled his iPod and a slip of paper from his pocket. "And umm, could you give her this? I have another one at home."

He held it out and wrinkled fingers took it from his hand.

"That's umm, my phone number. I mean, if she wanted to call, but, you know, she doesn't have to."

"I'll make sure she gets it."

"Thanks." He turned to the door and then paused. "How old is she?"

"Kelsy? Oh, about fifteen I should think."

Why wouldn't her own grandmother know for sure? Had Kelsy lied about her, about living here? If she didn't live here, where did she live? The way she always popped up out of nowhere he could almost believe she lived in the lake... but that was crazy.

He said goodbye to the old lady and made his way back to the car for the long drive home.


A few days later, Kelsy surfaced beside the jetty at Rebecca's cottage. She'd already been to the Vass house and the place was dark; the family was gone. Warm salty tears flowed down her cheek in a constant stream, but she'd sobbed and cried so much, sealed in her room, that she had no more left in her.

Rebecca sat outside in her wicker chair.

"Kelsy?"

Now a sob bubbled up and escaped as a strangled cough.

"What happened, child?" Rebecca approached the jetty and Kelsy pulled herself out of the water to sit on the deck.

"My mother..." she couldn't get the words out through the constriction in her throat.

"I am sorry. But it won't feel this way for ever." Rebecca sat beside her and put an arm around her shoulder. Kelsy leaned into her, feeling more love for the old woman than she ever thought she would be able to feel for her mother again.

"He came to see me," Rebecca said quietly.

"Was he mad I didn't come?"

"No. He was worried about you more than anything, maybe a little confused, and he didn't want to part with you. He cares about you a lot. Loves you even, dare I say it."

That tore the wound in her heart open afresh.

"He left a telephone number. And this."

Rebecca held out the iPod. Kelsy took it took it, twisted the headphone cable around her fingers and closed her eyes, thinking back to those days by the jetty sharing his music. Why did it have to be like this?

"He'll be back, child. And you know what they say; absence makes the heart grow fonder."

Yes. And stronger. She'd show her mother that, find a way to make her understand, and next summer things would be different.

# AUTHOR BIOGRAPHIES

The following author biographies reveal a little more about the people behind this book, and many include web links to the authors websites, blogs and more.

# John H. Barnes

Of my personal quest
into my haven of daytime dreams
where my uncomplicated yet complicated
and seemingly inexhaustible imagination waits.
A place where peace and solitude
that which I so longingly once viewed have left and gone astray.

Inspired as it was
from a script I was writing called
Yesterday's Invitation, it grew in my motherload
So desperately I needed to produce the poem,
adding it to the ever growing list
of published material of an author old enough to say

Known of a time I once knew as knowed.
Known from a time when knowed wasn't known
Now that age has grown to a point well won
The fifties aren't a time that was revered
now the sixties are an age I soon will revere,
looking to memories where my memory does dwell.

From England to Australia
And over all the lands in between
looking down from the plane gave new light
and a way to repeating those memories once seen
watching clouds that wander lonely as a dream
the plane split them as a typewriter splits words.

John lives and writes in West Australia. He has two published
novels, *The Demon Hunters* and *Return of the Demon Hunters* (now
out of print).

AUTHOR BIOGRAPHIES

## Andrew Campbell-Kearsey

Andrew Campbell-Kearsey is a writer living in Brighton. In another life he was a head teacher in London. His first collection of short stories *Brighton Shorts* was published in 2011 and he is currently working on his second novel. He gets his best ideas for writing while walking his dogs along the beach.

He is extremely excited about the transformation of some of his stories to the screen by Thorny Devil productions. He has won many competitions and his work can be found on his site www.andrewck.co.uk.

## Jim Cogan

Jim Cogan works as an IT Technician at one of the UK's leading Universities, is married and lives in his hometown of Bristol, UK, with wife, Debbie, and their two children James and Elliott.

He is a multi-instrumentalist and gigged through the mid-90's into the mid 2000's with numerous local rock and metal bands, then ran a part-time recording studio for local unsigned bands from 2005 to 2010.

Presently, when not working, looking after kids or doing seemingly endless piles of washing up at home, he still tries to find time to be creative. He enjoys writing fiction and screenplays, and still dabbles in a bit of music in his much reduced, home-based recording studio.

Also, he has begun to dabble in amateur film-making, initially focusing on music videos – you can read a blog of his latest film-making exploits on his film-making blog at www.mysticjim.blogspot.com.

He also presents movie themed podcast show called *The Crash and Burn Movie Podcast*, which you can check out at www.crashandburnmoviepodcast.co.uk.

## Amy Cummins

Amy loves horror, cartoons and animals - but not altogether - and has been writing poetry since she was 13. She has a weakness for dark chocolate, crisps and milkshakes, and an inexplicable fear of clowns.

Originally from Kent, Amy now lives near Bristol with her husband, Mark and children Chloe and Leon. She can often be found at comic conventions with Hellbound Media and The Great Escape. She is a breastfeeding peer supporter and a volunteer for the National Childbirth Trust.

## Troy Dennison

Troy is a professional make-up artist, writer, actor, artist and XBox junkie.

He published his first story *Monsters Are Real* in the eZine *13 Human Souls* and has since gone on to publish several short stories and his first novel *Hunters*. He is the creator of the *Tales From The Lounge* and *Dragon Days* web-comics. He is currently completing his second novel *After Dark*.

Troy has a background in art and theatre and trained as a make-up artist. Troy has worked on music videos, in theatre and independent film. As an actor Troy has found himself working opposite his own make-up creations on several occasions. His independent film credits include the movies *The Clown*, *Checking In* and *Furor*. His interest in films grew from an early age, influenced by *Star Wars: A New Hope* and stories his great-uncle would tell him about classic monster movies like *King Kong* and *Dracula*.

Troy was born and grew up in Staffordshire where he still resides with his three children, and crazy dog Theo.

# Damian Garside

Damian Garside is a British-born poet and academic residing permanently in South Africa with his wife Modiegi. Born in 1953 (Chinese Snake year) he lectures in Media And Communication in the university town of Mafikeng, having been educated at Manchester University and the University of Cape Town (where he received his doctorate in 1998). He teaches and researches cultural and media theory, film and scriptwriting. He is interested in science, philosophy and military history.

He loves reading, sci-fi film and TV, the Downfall parodies, South Park, Chris Rock, Trevor Noah, Sascha Baron Cohen, Jemaine Clement, Nice Peter, Manchester United and the San Francisco 49ers. His favourite poets and writers include William Blake, Ezra Pound, Alexander Pope, Milan Kundera, Gunter Grass, Arundhati Roy, Jonathan Swift, J.M.Coetzee, T.S. Eliot, Artur Rimbaud and James Joyce.

He has had poetry published in major South African poetry journals and anthologies since the early 1980s. In May this year he started tweeting poems and set up a poetry blog which you can find at damian2649.wordpress.com.

# Christopher M. Geeson

Christopher M. Geeson's short fiction includes Love Thy Spider in Dark Tales: Volume 12; Punchbag in The British Fantasy Society Journal: Autumn 2011; and a story in the forthcoming Steampunk Cthulhu anthology. His script, The Job Interview, was produced for industry showcases at ITV and Channel 4. A big fan of alternative music, he has had fifty reviews printed in magazines and local press. 2013 will see him concentrating on more short stories and an epic children's fantasy adventure novel.

Christopher lives with his partner, Manda, in North Yorkshire, where he works in schools, running creative workshops for children. For more info on these workshops, search for him on www.creativenorthyorkshire.com.

# Heidi Hovis

Heidi is a mother to three biological and three step children. She lives in central Alberta, Canada where she writes and stays home to raise her brood. Having grown up with a mother who worked in a Native School she has always had an interest and passion for their legends, myths and culture. The Cardinal Ruins came from that passion as well as an interest in writing about paranormal and supernatural themes. She is presently working on full length novels in the hopes of publishing one in the near future.

# Sophie Jackson

Sophie Jackson has worked as a journalist and writer since 2003 and has been published in various anthologies. Her day-job involves writing articles for various magazines and papers including the *Daily Mirror* and she also writes history books for The History Press and Fonthill Media. She is also the author of the *Clara Fitzgerald Mysteries*, murder mysteries set in 1920s Brighton which are exclusive to Amazon Kindle. You can learn more about her at www.sophie-jackson.co.uk.

# T. James

T. James came late to the world of poetry and fiction writing, his creativity having been buried for 25 years under a lab coat, Fat Cat business suit, and a hospital therapist's uniform.

At the present time he is perfecting his ability to bend the written word to his will across a range of genres, styles, and forms. He has wheezed his way up the knoll of the novella, squeezed through the constriction of non-fiction, and breezed to rest in the tepee of poetry before he found a big enough word-shovel to dig out a novel.

He continues to believe that "X" marks the spot, but wonders why every treasure map is upside down, no matter which way he turns it. You can follow his excavations at http://thewordonthe.net.

# Patti Ludwig

Patti Ludwig lives on the Pacific Coast of North America with a cat. Her internal editor is in constant need of slapping down, and she hangs out at a few fantasy author internet boards. She persists in re-reading a number of books people think she should have memorized, and she crochets sometimes unexpected items that she can't sell. Riverchild is her first published short story.

# Drew Moffatt

Drew Moffatt is an amateur writer, originally from South Wales and now living in southwest England. This is his first published story and was written specifically for The Great Escape. He hopes one day to become a struggling genre fiction writer.

# Sabine Naus

Sabine Naus lives and writes in Canada. Her story *The Christmas Tights* was runner up in The Great Escape's 2011 Christmas writing contest.

# Emma Scott

Emma Scott is a young writer and relatively new to the world of writing, although she has been creating stories since before she could pen the words. When she is not busy scribbling in her journal or on pads of paper, she enjoys playing and teaching piano and flute, and being creative with a needle and thread. She lives in Reading, England with her parents and four younger brothers.

## J. D. Waye

J Dianne Waye lives and writes in Canada, the setting for several of her novels and short stories. Most of her stories include a supernatural element, but her first love will always be science fiction. Her story, *Sagarmatha*, was conceived while researching mountain-climbing for a novel, and – of course – by Jeff's photo.

## Andy Whitson

Andy Whitson was born in Edinburgh and he is older than he thinks he is. He and his wife live in Niedersachsen, Germany with their cat Philip. He spends his playtime writing, getting lost in music, drawing, painting and being as child-like as possible.

## Gareth Wilson

Life is certainly something of interest, especially when you share it with four felines who rule the house with paws of iron. Add to this the demands of a very cheeky monkey (she who shall not be named) and all round quirky situations which arise, and you have many thoughts for the writers "What If?" pile. When I'm not administering to the demands of those around, I can usually be found with my nose in a book or looking at a blank page trying to get my thoughts out. Life, in the North-West of England is definitely stranger than fiction.

## Kat-in-the-Attic (Illustrator)

Kat Wilson is an illustrator from the North of England. From the first time she read a fairytale and then later when she became engrossed in the Hobbit, Kat has been a fond lover of the way word and image work together to create works of great fiction. When she later in life she discovered comics, it seemed the perfect fit for her love of combining art and writing. She now creates her own comics, illustrates for books and creates props and costumes in the Attic while occasionally coming out to make a cup of tea and possibly have cake. You can find out more about her work and projects at www.kat-in-the-attic.com.

## Chrissey Harrison (Editor)

Chrissey Harrison is fiction editor and principle contributor at *The Great Escape*, a website offering escapist entertainment. If allowed to consider writing as her profession, she would say her hobbies are film making and photography. Her published works include short novella *The Star Coin Prophecy*, and two adult short stories published with Naughty Nights Press. She lives in Cardiff, UK, with her partner and a lot of fish.

Find out more at chrisseysgreatescape.wordpress.com